THE ADVENTURES OF

THE 31st STREET SAINTS

J. A. McKINSTRY

BOOK 1: THE ENO

THE ADVENTURES OF THE 31st STREET SAINTS

J. A. McKINSTRY

BOOK 1: THE ENO

Tate Publishing & *Enterprises*

Published by Tate Publishing & Enterprises, LLC
127 E. Trade Center Terrace | Mustang, Oklahoma 73064 USA
1.888.361.9473 | www.tatepublishing.com

Tate Publishing is committed to excellence in the publishing industry. The company reflects the philosophy established by the founders, based on Psalms 68:11,
"The Lord gave the word and great was the company of those who published it."

Cover design by Elizabeth Mason
Interior design by Janae J. Glass

Published in the United States of America

ISBN: 978-1-5988689-2-x
07.04.05

This book is dedicated to the love of my life, my wife Lynnie, to my two children, Mari and Garrett, who daily inspire and bring joy to my life, and to my parents, Ron and Shirley, who guided me on the path to my Lord and Savior, Jesus Christ.

Introduction

In the tiny seaside town of Chewela, somewhere in the Great Pacific Northwest, unusual stirrings were occurring at the Saint Barnabus the Munificent Cathedral.

The revered Cardinal Eslaf Tehporp, affectionately called, Cardinal Essey, had established a "Spiritual Cleansing" experience for the youth of the town. These cleansings were his way, he would say, to help guide the youth on the path of righteousness. The townspeople, young and old, were cleverly deceived into believing this lie. Everyone that is, except for Jojo, Hooch, Jill and Gus, four orphans residing in the Saint Barnabus All Saints Orphanage at the end of town, on 31st Street. They knew differently. These four children, who secretly referred to themselves as the 31st Street Saints, were passionately determined to expose the Cardinal and his devious plan of terror and hopelessness.

The All Saints Orphanage

Once, not so long ago, there were four orphans named Jojo, Hooch, Gus and Jill. They lived in the sleepy seaside town of Chewela, somewhere in the Great Pacific Northwest. As orphans, with no living or willing relative to care for them, they resided in the All Saints Orphanage on 31st Street. The orphanage was owned and managed by Saint Barnabus the Munificent Cathedral, which also controlled the town.

Life at the orphanage was hard and unpleasant. The rules were strict and heavily enforced by Priests of little compassion. If rules were broken, punishment was swift and severe. Rarely was any praise given, and the only source of comfort was close friends. Kids had to band together, to "watch out for each other's backs," so to speak. Survival at the orphanage depended on it. Jojo, Hooch, Gus, and Jill were just such kids. They stuck closely together, and secretly referred to themselves as the, 31st Street Saints. This is their story.

"Sssshhhhh, quiet!" hushed Jojo. He put a finger to his lips for added emphasis. "If the *It* hears you, you may be next."

Upon hearing the command, the boys in Room 7 of the dormitory on Level 2, Section B, pulled their one ratty blanket up to their chins, and made like they were fast asleep. All, that is, except for one rather large, muscular eleven year-old named, Hooch. He was fast asleep and snoring like a freight train. The covers on his bed had been kicked onto the floor, exposing the words No Fear on his t-shirt. The command for quiet caused him to stir. Sitting up abruptly and rubbing his eyes, he mumbled, "I didn't do it! I promise!" He then rolled back over fast asleep.

Five-year-old twin boys, Lou and Bob, and ten-year old Gus, obeyed and squeezed their eyes tightly shut, as the door creaked slowly open. The hallway light cast an eerie shadow over an enormous figure, which remained motionless in the doorway.

This *It*, as the orphans dubbed this insidious creature, was the powerful High Priest of the St. Barnabus the Munificent Cathedral. The dubious title, *It,* was given because of the black hooded, full-length robe that was worn. Covering the *Its'* face as it did, gave the wicked High Priest the appearance of something ghostly and evil, someone or some '*thing*' to be feared.

The *It* handled all disciplinary affairs for Cardinal Eslaf Tehporp, affectionately referred to by his parishioners as Cardinal Essey, the powerful leader of the St. Barnabus Congregation. The *It* was always on and about the business of the Cardinal, and the business tonight brought the *It* to Room 7.

After pausing briefly in the doorway, the *It* began to move around the room. For someone or *something* of such enormous size, the *It* moved with astonishing ease, grace and purpose. Creaks from the ancient floorboards could be heard every so often, as the *It* moved between the beds, glancing downwards every so often. The smell of liquor and onions, an awful stench, caused the children to gag. Carefully, they pulled the blankets over their mouth and nostrils. The *It* passed by their beds to Jojo's.

Arriving at the foot of Jojo's bed, the *It* reached down and carefully removed the clipboard that hung at the end of his bed. This clipboard contained information regarding Jojo's age, year of arrival to the orphanage, method of arrival, and so forth. Through squinted eyes, Jojo watched as the *It* perused his chart.

He'd seen this enormous individual before; smelled the vile entity, too. He just couldn't remember where. Flowing about in that ghostly black robe and smelling as the *It* did was a hard image to forget. And here the *It* was, standing at the end of his bed.

After what seemed an eternity, but was in fact only a minute or two, the *It* uttered words that resonated as if from the bottom of a deep well, "Soon, very soon." Then, very deftly, the chart was hung back on the bed rail, as the *It* exited the room. There was a collective sigh of relief among the Saints as the door creaked shut behind the black robed monstrosity.

Jojo was to turn thirteen on May 8. Today was the 6TH. Birthdays, especially one's thirteenth, were not days to be celebrated at the All Saints Orphanage. They were days to dread. Just ask Gus Leibowitz, whose brother Eddie Leibowitz celebrated his yesterday.

"Jojo," stammered Gus, "the *It* is going to take you just like Eddie—and in two days. We can't let this happen, we just can't!" he said as his eyes began to well up.

Gus and Eddie had been in and out of foster homes as many times as their dad had been in and out of prison. A meth lab explosion had left their mother dead, and their dad was still doing hard time in the Walla Walla State Penitentiary. Gus couldn't even remember what he looked like.

Lou and Bob jumped out of bed and tackled Jojo. They hadn't spoken a word since their arrival to St. Barnabus. No one knew why. They just didn't talk. They spoke by being physical. The tackle was their way of expressing their love.

"Hey, get off of me!" yelled Jojo, in mock anger.

The twins paid no attention; they were having too much fun. They continued roughing him up, as the other Saints just laughed. Jojo was like a father to them. He was the reason they were still alive.

They had been left on the doorsteps of the orphanage, in a card board box by an unwed teenage mother, in the darkness of winter. One thin blanket was all that sheltered the twins from the cold. It was unclear how long they had remained on the steps before being discovered. They never cried, so no one took any notice. That happened a lot at the orphanage; things went unnoticed.

No one at the orphanage ever checked the front door. Only packages and parcels came that way. Items like that were rare commodities at the 31st Street Orphanage.

If not for Jojo's keen eye, checking one morning to see if the snow falling was heavy enough to close school for the day, the twins would have died of exposure. A special bond between them had existed ever since.

"Back in bed you two, or I'll knock you out!" he said, with a growl.

The twins jumped back into bed with a smile.

All of the commotion had done something that thunderstorm's and earthquake's had never been able to accomplish. It woke up Hooch.

"What's going on?!" he slurred, wiping drool from his cheek. "Is it time for breakfast, already?"

Everyone laughed as Jojo threw his pillow across the room. It hit Hooch squarely in the face, causing him to moan in mock pain.

"Owww! I've been hit! Oh, the pain, the *excruciating* pain! Help! Quick! Call 911!"

Hooch didn't fool anyone, especially Lou and Bob. They burst into laughter, along with Jojo and Gus. They knew he wasn't hurt. Nothing, as far as they were concerned, could ever hurt a rock like Hooch. Though a year younger than Jojo, Hooch had been at the orphanage the longest.

Severely abused, both physically and emotionally by his parents, Hooch was taken from his home, a run-down trailer in the back woods where they lived, by Chewela Child Protective Service workers. They made the call for his removal from the home because of persistent calls by neighbors of loud screams and crying, and school reports of bruises and scrapes covering his body. Thick welts from a tree branch, used to beat him, were still evident across the small of his back. A scar from an angry fist, below his left eye that required thirteen stitches, seemed to dance on his face with each smile. His parents skipped town before going to court to face charges. No one knew their whereabouts, and fewer cared.

"Yeah," Hooch would say. "Good riddance!"

Though happy to be away from his abusive parents, once in the care of the state, things just got worse. Moving to and from foster homes with record setting regularity created in him a violent temper. He didn't love or trust anyone. He had become one of those children in the system deemed unsalvageable. A year later, after unsuccessfully moving from foster home to foster home, he was sent where all incorrigibles go, those failures in the Chewela Foster Care System for whom there is no hope: the All Saints Orphanage.

Too young to be on his own and with no worthy or accepting relative to care for him, the orphanage took in the tough street waif under the guise of compassion. There were definite reasons why this particular orphanage took kids in, but compassion was not one of them. The 31st Street Saints would soon discover the real reason. Why others before them hadn't was a mystery. For now, though, Hooch needed some clarification on a different matter.

"No, I'm serious. Really, what's up?" he asked.

"The *It* was here," said Gus in a somber tone, "while you were sleeping."

"The *It* was here, *tonight*!?" he shouted, looking over at Eddie's empty bed. "Not again. Who was taken this time?" he said, scanning the room to see if anyone else was missing.

Jojo looked his way and gave him a wink.

"Hey, wait a minute," said Hooch, with a smile. "I forgot. It's *your* birthday in a couple of days. Whew! I'm glad I'm not looking at *your* empty bed. Oh, and sorry about that. I've always been a sound sleeper."

"*We know*!" chimed in Jojo and Gus.

"Why did the *It* come early?" asked Hooch. "I mean your birthday *is* a couple of days off, right?"

"Yeah...the beast came early, all right, and I think I might know why."

"Yeah, why's that?" asked Gus.

"Well," he began, "you know how Eddie was taken and we never woke up or heard anything?"

"Yeah, that was weird," said Hooch, "but...what about it?"

Jojo went on to explain how on the eve of Eddie's disappearance, the vitamins that all orphans are required to take every night—to help keep them healthy so that they won't get sick and cost the church needless money, as the Priests would say—were not vitamins at all. They were sleeping pills.

"What?!" yelled Hooch.

At which point Gus reminded him that the *It* was still lurking about.

"How do you know that? They sure looked like the vitamins to me."

At dinner, the night of Eddie's disappearance, Jojo said he overheard some of the orphans from Level 1. They were talking about how they were going to be getting some 'fresh meat' real soon. He shuddered as he spoke.

"Just the thought of turning thirteen and having to go down to Level 1 gives me the creeps," Jojo said.

"Yeah, those older kids make my skin crawl," said Gus. "Even the ones from our room that we used to like have become so strange."

"I know what you mean," added Hooch, "those empty, lifeless eyes. It's like they're there, but they're not. Even guys like Tank and BJ who I liked and stuck up for when they lived with us act like I don't even exist."

"Yeah," added Gus. "They act weird and dress weird. Those tacky bracelets they have to wear. I mean, what's up with that?"

"And all of this," said Jojo, "has something to do with the *It*. I can't quite put my finger on why, but I believe that monster is at the bottom of this. No question."

"Oh, you can bank on that!" declared Hooch in a seething tone. "If there's a key to what's going on in this dung heap, you can bet the *It* is involved in a major way."

Among the many different facets that made up Horatio Q.Tuckett, aka, Hooch, was his violent temper. It tended to get the best of him from time to time, especially if he felt he or a friend of his was wronged in some way. And it was at one particular meal that his unruly temper reared its ugly head.

It was just yesterday at lunch, when one of the older Level 1 boys acted rudely towards Jill. She had just gotten her lunch and was rounding a corner on her way to sit with Hooch and the other Room 7 kids.

"Nice butt," the boy had said, reaching out and grabbing her roughly and *very* inappropriately. Hooch saw what happened. The only thing the boy saw was the straight right that knocked him and his two front teeth clean out. That perfectly placed punch landed Hooch in the Hole for a cold, cramped and lonely night of solitary confinement with only stale bread and water for comfort.

"After you're through freezing for the night," hissed the *It*, unseen from beneath his hood, "you can plan on kitchen duty for the next two weeks, as well!"

Hooch would say later that it was well worth it—even the extra kitchen duty. But his thoughts turned once again to his best friend's upcoming birthday.

"JoJo," Hooch said, in a tone so serious that everyone leaned closer to listen. "We just lost Eddie. You're up next, and I'm in the bullpen. We've got to put a stop to this. We've got to find out what's going on here."

All eyes fell on Jojo. Like Hooch, Jojo was very tough; unlike Hooch, he was better at controlling his temper...not that he didn't have one, mind you. It's just that a record setting number of consecutive times in the Hole over the first year of his internment at the orphanage had made him a bit wiser.

Jojo arrived to the orphanage after the death of his parents two years ago. Before the tragic train wreck that took both of their lives, he had what he referred to as the perfect life—the best parents imaginable, and not a care in the world. That horrific accident changed his life in an instant.

"It was the worst day of my life," said Jojo, upon hearing of the death of his parents as a ten-year-old child. His arrival to the orphanage was the second.

"My dad was an Elder in the Saint Barnabas the Munificent Cathedral almost up until his untimely death. Because St.Barnabus owns and operates the All Saints Orphanage, the Elders, Priests, and even Cardinal Essey felt it would be fair and just that I be given the privilege of living here; that and the fact that I had no other living relatives to take me in."

At the word "privilege," Hooch made a gagging sound like he was throwing up. The twins howled with delight.

"Yeah, *privilege*...riiiiiggggght," was all Gus could muster.

The question came up as to how his parents were killed.

"Yeah," asked Hooch. "And what did you mean by your dad being an Elder *almost* up until he was killed? Did he quit or something?'

"Now that, and a few other mysterious incidents, is where this whole story gets interesting," answered Jojo. "Would you like to hear it?"

All five roommates chimed in with an emphatic "*Yes*!" as they scooched closer to Jojo.

They did keep in mind to use soft voices, though, as the *It* might still be lurking about.

The Story

As Jojo was beginning to tell his story, the doorknob began to slowly turn.

"The *It*!" Jojo exclaimed, as all of the Saints dove back to their beds, and made like they were fast asleep.

As the door creaked open a quiet voice whispered, "Hey Guys! It's me! The coast is clear!"

"Jill!" yelled Hooch, as everyone motioned for him to be quiet. "What are you doing here?"

"Yeah," added Gus. "If you're caught, you'll be in a world of hurt. No girls are allowed in the boy's dorm, you know that."

"I know, I know! I just missed you guys," she said as she plopped down on the edge of Hooch's bed. "Besides, my dorm room has some really creepy kids in it. I had to get out of there."

"Well, I'm glad you're here," said Hooch, as he gently took hold of her hand. "I missed you, too."

"Oh, man…I think I'm gonna be sick," said Gus. "And let go of my sister, will you!?"

"Oh, quiet, little brother," Jill said with a smile, as she made a fist like she was going to throw a punch.

"Hey, Gus," laughed Hooch. "You better shut up or she'll knock you out!"

"Enough, already!" interjected Jojo. "Will you two cut it out? If it's okay with everyone, I'd like to finish my story. Now, gather around and be quiet about it. Remember, if Jill's caught, it's off to the Hole with her for sure."

Everyone nodded in agreement as they shuffled quickly and quietly to Jojo's bed. They were all ears as he began his story.

"It all started," he began, "about two and a half years ago this coming Thursday. The newly elected, Mayor Nomed Epop, declared every Thursday to be set aside for what he called, Youth Atonement Day. It was his desire to impress upon the youth of Chewela the need for forgiveness and spiritual cleansing. The European born High Cardinal, Eslaf Tehporp, affectionately called, Cardinal Essey by his parishioners, was required to be there, as more than just a journeyman Priest was needed for this special kind of atonement. My dad was still an Elder at that time, and he and the other Elders thought all of this a very good idea, especially the part about having someone so powerful in the ministry as the Cardinal overseeing the event. With, as my dad would later say, "the wayward youth of today needing some guidance," this Youth Atonement Day was just the ticket. Everyone in Chewela bought into it hook, line and sinker."

"No pun intended, but it all sounds pretty fishy to me," said Hooch.

"I agree," Jill said with a nod.

Gus was getting antsy about the rest of the story.

"Keep going," he pleaded. "This is getting interesting!"

"Very well," continued Jojo. "Now, where was I? Oh, yes," he went on, "hook, line and sinker…"

He continued to explain how his dad and the other Elders would assist Cardinal Essey, from 7:00 p.m. to 9:00 p.m. every Thursday evening, along with a handful of specially sanctified Priests referred to as the Cardinal's Truly Blessed Priests, whatever that meant. The High Priest—the *It*—the Cardinal's ever-present personal assistant, was in attendance, as well.

"On Thursday evenings," Jojo continued, "kids would be brought to the Cathedral, and lined up on the front steps. The Priests would escort them into the Cardinal's Sanctified Chambers for cleansing in the order of their arrival. Parents tried to get there early, as the entire evening of cleansing lasted for only two hours. With hundreds of churchgoers wanting to participate, there was a real possibility of waiting all that time, and never getting an audience with the Cardinal."

"Waiting in line all the time for nothing," said Jill. "That sounds awful."

"I know what you mean," answered Jojo. "But the people didn't seem to care. The number of eager participants was so enormous that the line could be seen snaking many blocks away, clear around the massive cathedral grounds."

"Hey," said Hooch, "I don't remember seeing them lined up like that? How'd I miss that?"

"Probably because you were in the Hole, while the rest of us were washing floors, doing dishes, or locked in our rooms," quipped Gus, with a smile.

"Good call," smiled Hooch.

"Now," said Jojo with an irritated edge in his voice,

"we're running out of nighttime. Would anyone object to my continuing?"

"Yes, yes, yes," answered Hooch, "*soooooo* sorry."

Jojo smiled and then continued, by briefly explaining about the Cardinal's Sanctified Chambers. It was in this room that only the High Cardinal Essey and his Truly Blessed Priests were allowed to enter.

"And, of course, those poor fool kids chosen to be cleansed, right?" asked Hooch.

"Yes," said Jojo. "And it's said that there is a special chair in the room that the Cardinal uses for the cleansing."

"What kind of chair?" asked Gus.

"It's rumored," Jojo went on to say, "that this special or 'Anointed Chair' is one that only the High Cardinal is permitted to sit on. If anyone else were to sit on it, including the *It* or any other Priests, legend has it that they would immediately burst into flames."

"Riiiiggghhtt!" mocked Hooch. "You're kidding, *aren't* you?"

"I wish I was," continued Jojo, as he described the history of the chair that his father passed on to him before his death.

"Not only is it the truth, " he continued, "but it's written in the cathedral archives that this is the same chair that was used in the early cleansing of the church; as far back as the 1300's. Those people who didn't agree with, and believe in the church doctrines—heathens, if you will, were strapped to the chair and consumed by flames."

"Yuck," said Gus. "What a way to go."

"Yeah, and get this," continued Jojo. "After all of the fire that this chair has been through, it is still unscathed and perfectly in tact. No scorch marks, smell of fire, nothing!"

"How come the Cardinal doesn't flame on like everyone else?" asked Hooch.

"My father," said Jojo, "told me of a powerful spiritual being named, Natas, who somehow empowered the Cardinal with more power than the chair itself."

"Natas?" asked the Saint's in unison. "Who's that?"

"Better, yet," said Hooch, "is he still around?"

"No one knows for sure, but the cathedral archives refer to a special prison somewhere that Natas has been in for a very long time. Cardinal Essey is the only one that knows where that prison is, and when Natas will be released."

"Sounds like an important person to me. Must be some kind of prison to keep an individual like that locked up," said Jill, in a more serious tone.

"That's for sure," Jojo replied.

"Maybe this guy, whoever he is, has the answer to what happened to your parents," said Gus.

"Could be," answered Jojo. "I do know that the *It*, the Cardinal, the Priests and all the rest, including the Underlings, are connected in some devious way."

"Under-*whos*?" asked Hooch. "I've never heard of them."

"Oh," continued Jojo, "that's just what I call the Level 1 Orphans. They seem to be *under* some sort of spell, or something. You even said yourself they seemed weird and lifeless, remember?

"Yeah, I guess," said Hooch. "I just never thought of it that way. Underlings...Hhhmmmmmm, that's good stuff."

"*Scary* stuff, really," Jojo answered. "But, now, where was I? Oh…yes…the process for getting an audience with the Cardinal."

Jojo went on to explain that once the youth arrived, they would wait in line with their parents. The line toward the Chambers of Cardinal Essey inched forward, slowly making its way through the dark halls of the Cathedral to an alcove located across from the entrance to the Sanctified Chambers. It was there, in a holding area of sorts, that they waited until it was their turn to enter.

Each youth, as it came their turn to meet with the Cardinal, would leave their parents, and remain with an attending Priest. Once the parents left and went down to the foray at the entrance of the cathedral to wait, the kids would then enter the Sanctified Chambers with a hooded Priest."

"Hey," asked Hooch, "how come you know so much about this, anyway?"

"Many nights as a little kid," Jojo began, "while my dad was in closed meetings with the Elders and the Cardinal, he would leave me with Father Lead-bottom."

"Lead-*What*?" exclaimed Gus.

"Lead-bottom…well…that's what *I* called him," said Jojo with a laugh. "I don't know what his real name was, but he had this enormous, I mean *gargantuan*, butt. He sat around way too much, and it just sort of grew—*huge*! Anyway, I would tell him I was going to the restroom, and would just conveniently never come back. He was too lazy and fat to come looking for me. I would spend the rest of the time roaming around the cathedral, hiding and spying on the Priests. It was great fun."

"What did you see?" asked Hooch. "Did you see any cleansing?"

"Well, as I was saying, one night after leaving Lead-bottom, I began roaming the cathedral. I'm not really sure, but I did find, or rather stumbled onto, a back entrance that led to the Sanctified Chambers."

"Really?" asked Gus, leaning forward ever so slightly. "How did that happen?"

"Well, it all happened by chance, luck, if you will. I was walking past the Cardinal's Chambers, when I noticed two Priests coming toward me. I ducked across the hallway behind a low stone wall near the alcove."

"Yikes! Then what?" asked Gus.

"As soon as they passed by, I thought I heard some talking coming from the Chambers, so I crept out from behind the alcove and inched my way across the hallway to the door."

"Could you make out the voices?" asked Gus.

"Yes," answered Jojo. "With my ear to the door, I heard voices, *very* familiar voices."

"Who were they?" asked Gus, again.

"I was almost positive that the voices of two of the men were my father's and Cardinal Essey's. I'm not completely certain, but I think the third was Mayor Epop."

"Any others?" asked Jill.

"Yes, a woman's," said Jojo. "It was my mother. I'm sure of it."

"Whoa," said Gus, "your *mother*? Why would she be there?"

"That's just it. She wasn't supposed to be," continued Jojo. "She must have arrived around the time I was being entertained by old Lead-bottom."

"Could you hear anything?" asked Hooch.

"Yes, I could hear arguing, lots of it! Then, out of nowhere, a blaze of light flashed under the door out into the hallway. Screams of pain and agony could be heard," Jojo said. "Then everything went quiet, deathly quiet. The loudest sound I heard was the thumping of my heart."

"You saw light?" asked Gus. "I wonder if kids waiting in line ever noticed it."

"Good thinking," said Jojo. "But remember, each youth waiting next in line, would have to wait *away* from the Cardinal's Chambers, with a Priest to escort them. So, it would be almost impossible for them to see or hear anything until it was their turn."

"And from the sounds of those screams, too late, as well." said Hooch.

"Okay, okay," said Gus impatiently. "After the light and screams, then what happened?"

"The door started to open," continued Jojo, "so I hustled outta there and hid behind the stone wall near the alcove."

He paused, took a deep breath, and continued.

"As the door opened a huge figure in a black hooded robe rushed out and headed, fortunately for me, in the other direction."

"The *It*!" shouted Gus and Hooch in unison. "It had to be!"

"*That's* where you remember seeing the beast!" exclaimed Jill.

"You're right, it had to be. I'm sure of it," continued JoJo. "I didn't get a clear look at the High Priest's face, but who does behind that black hooded robe? But that smell. *Whew*!! Definitely liquor and onions! No question, even from across the hallway!"

"Did the *It* see you?" asked Hooch.

"No, I was startled into moving backwards, though, which was not good thing for me," said Jojo. "I caught my heel on the edge of the top stair next to the alcove where I was hiding. I tripped backwards, tumbling down to the bottom of the stairwell."

"Ouch! Rough landing," said Hooch. "What happened next?"

"I was a bit groggy from the fall, and was hoping the *It* hadn't heard anything. I reached for anything to get a hold of to pull myself up, and grabbed on to a decorative gargoyle at the bottom of the stairs," said Jojo. "When I pulled myself up, the gargoyle came down like a lever. Two huge stones next to me opened inwards, just enough of an opening for me to step through."

"A secret passageway!" exclaimed Gus.

"Did you go in?" asked Hooch, leaning forward ever so slightly.

"Heck, yeah!" answered Jojo. "I didn't know if the *It* heard me fall, and I wasn't planning on waiting to find out. I moved as quickly as I could."

"What happened then?" asked Gus.

"As I let the gargoyle go," Jojo continued, "it moved back to its upright position. Then, after stepping inside, the stones closed behind me. I was alone, on the other side of the stairway, trapped in the dark."

"What did you do then?" asked Hooch.

"Off in the distance was a light," Jojo continued. "I inched my way along the side of the narrow corridor that curved off to the left. There were voices off in that direction, so I kept going. I followed the sound of the voices, which lead me right to a stairway, about fifty feet away."

"Did you go up the stairs?" they asked.

"Yes. As I made my way up the stairs, the voices I heard became clearer; but the arguing had stopped. As I reached the top step, there was a thick red curtain covering the entrance to the doorway. The voices became very clear, and neither of them was my mother's or father's."

"Did you get a look inside?" asked Gus.

"I listened for a second or two then worked up the courage to peek in. As I did I heard what had to be the Cardinal's voice say something like, 'Your wife was first, and now it's your turn.' I opened the curtain just a crack, when it happened."

"*What* happened?!" asked Hooch, almost in a shout.

"I caught a glimpse of my dad being held by two Priests in front of someone sitting in the Sanctified Chair. He was seated in such a way, with a Priest blocking my view, that at first I couldn't see his face. By the clothing and robes and rings that I did see, I *knew* it must be the Cardinal."

"Who else could it have been?" asked Gus.

"No one, you're right," continued Jojo. "And what happened next is something I will never forget."

"What was it?" asked Jill, who noticed Jojo's face going a bit pale. "Are you all right?"

"I'll be fine," he answered, pausing for a minute. He took a deep breath and continued. "I noticed that my dad had tape over his mouth, and his hands were tied behind his back. He was wiggling and struggling to get away, as two large hooded Priests held him tightly. As he twisted and turned, he looked my way. Our eyes met for a millisecond.

He looked terrified. And then, right before a flash of light exploded in the room, I saw why."

"*Why*!?" asked Hooch. "What was it?'

"I don't know for sure," continued Jojo, "and it may have been the light exploding as it did that caused me to see things. But, as my father jerked about to get free, he forced the Priests to move giving me a clear view of the Cardinal, or *whatever* it was that was sitting there."

"What do you mean, *whatever,* it was?" asked Gus. "Was it the Cardinal, or not?"

"What I mean," said Jojo, "is that it was the Cardinal's body, but…but…"

"But *what*?!" shouted Hooch. "What was it that was so terrifying?"

"It, or the Cardinal, had a…a…"

"A *what*?!" yelled Jill. "*What*!?"

"A snake's head, all right!? I said it!" shouted Jojo. "He had the *body* of a man and the *head* of a snake!"

The Saints froze. No one moved. No one spoke. It was almost too much for any of them to absorb. It was Gus who finally broke the silence.

"Are you sure?" he asked. "I mean, you *were* in quite a predicament. Do you think maybe your eyes were playing tricks on you?"

"No…no…" said Jojo. "I've thought about it a lot; had a lot of nightmares about it, too. It was a snake's head. And, it, or the Cardinal, hissed as it spoke. That forked tongue shooting out like it did was hideous."

"Wow," was all Jill could say, as she gave him a hug. "No wonder your father was so frightened. Who wouldn't be?"

"And there's more," continued Jojo, taking a deep breath and gathering himself the best he could. "As my father was struggling with the Priests, one of their hoods fell off exposing the same thing, a *snake's* head! And then the light exploded! The brilliance, though muted somewhat by the curtain, blinded me enough to force me backwards losing my balance. I was just able to catch the top stair rail. "

"Lucky you," said Gus. "How'd you finally get out of there?"

"As I said, I stumbled but managed to hold onto the side rail, and slowly work my way to the bottom of the stairs. By the time I reached the last step, my vision was starting to clear. I inched my way back to the entrance, and began looking and feeling for a gargoyle or some lever to pull—but there was nothing. Fortunately, there didn't need to be."

"What do you mean?" asked Jill.

"Well," continued Jojo, "as I reached the end of the passageway, my weight landing on two stones on the floor must have triggered the stones in the wall to move. The secret door just opened on its own."

"What did you do then?" asked Hooch.

"I ran home as fast as I could, and hid in my room," he said, his eyes beginning to well up with tears. "I crawled into my bed, and lay there, waiting for my parents to come home. I knew in my heart they weren't coming, but I stayed awake as long as I could. Then I just fell asleep. I didn't wake up until I heard a knock on the front door the next morning."

"Then wha…?" Hooch began to ask, as they all went silent. The knob of their room door was slowly being turned.

"Quick! Back to bed!" urged Jojo. "Jill, hide under Hooch's bed!" She did just that, and quickly scampered under his bed which was the farthest away from the door.

The quick patter of soft feet subsided just as the door opened. All of the Saints made as if they were fast asleep, with Jill motionless beneath Hooch's bed. Then, as mysteriously as the door had been opened, it closed.

After a minute or two, Hooch leaned over and gave the all clear sign to Jill. She crawled out from under the bed, and hurried to the door. Carefully, opening the door, she peaked out into the hallways which, thankfully, were empty. Then, turning back, she gave a thumb's up that it was safe to leave. With a wave and a smile, she disappeared into the dark, silent corridors of the orphanage.

Room 7 went silent for the night.

More of the Story

At daybreak a sliver of sunlight, flickering through a tear in a window shade, cut across the room. The door opened abruptly, as the Morning Duty Priest made his usual gruff announcement.

"*Everybody up*! *Breakfast in ten minutes*!"

The door slammed behind him. The Saints stretched, moaned, and groaned doing everything possible to wake up. Finally awake, they made their way into the bathroom. Once their hair was combed and teeth brushed, they went out the door and into the chow line, which curved its' way down steps leading past the infamous Level 1 area where the Underlings lived, and into the cafeteria for breakfast.

Hooch glanced over in the direction of the girl's dormitory, hoping to catch a glimpse of Jill. He saw her coming. A huge smile crossed his face, as he paused momentarily, waiting to make sure she saw him. She did. She smiled back.

"*Keep moving*!" shouted the Cafeteria Priest, as a push

from behind moved Hooch forward. "*Fill your plate, sit down, and eat*!" he bellowed again.

All orphans, both girls and boys, were permitted to congregate together during meals. After filling their plates, Jojo, Hooch, Jill, and Gus made their way to a section of the cafeteria as far away from the Underlings as possible.

"Hi, Jill," said Hooch with a smile.

"Hi you guys," she said, smiling back at Hooch as he managed to maneuver a seat right next to her.

"Oh, isn't that sweet?" teased Gus. "Hoochie-Coochie and his little girlie friend."

Everyone laughed, Jill blushed, and Hooch nailed Gus in the forehead with a perfectly thrown sausage.

"Bulls eye!" said Hooch, quite pleased with his aim. "Now, shut up and let Jojo get on with his story. And give me that sausage back!" he shouted at Gus, who promptly plopped it in his mouth with a smile.

"Delicious!" he said, taunting Hooch playfully.

"All right, knock it off!" shouted Jojo. "And quit throwing food, or we'll all end up in the Hole."

Everyone agreed, as Jojo proceeded to continue the story. Gus was eager to help out.

"There was a knock on the door, right?" asked Gus.

"Right," said Jojo. "I was still kind of groggy and fuzzy-headed from all that had happened the night before. I was hoping that the knock on the door was just all part of a bad dream, or something. But I heard it again. I went down stairs and opened our front door. The local police and Priest Lead-bottom were there. They asked me to get dressed and go with them. I asked them why, but they wouldn't answer me. They just said that I would find out soon enough."

Jojo said that they drove him to the cathedral where Cardinal Essey was waiting. The Cardinal greeted the police with a great, big sanctimonious smile.

"He assured everyone," Jojo went on, "that I would be wonderfully taken care of. It was at that point that I asked where my parents were."

"How'd they answer that?' asked Jill.

"The way the Priests explained it to me, my dad needed to leave that night with my mom," said Jojo, "to attend some emergency meeting of the Saint Barnabus Council at headquarters, back east."

"Hadn't your dad already stepped down from being an Elder, because he disagreed with Cardinal Essey and all of the church doctrines?" asked Jill.

"Yes, that's correct," answered Jojo. "But the Cardinal made it sound like all was forgiven, and that my dad was to be reinstated; to become one of the head Elders again, a real high honor or something of the sort."

"Those liars!" blurted out Hooch. "You saw your dad in the Sanctified Chambers!"

"Exactly," continued Jojo. "And my dad never would have given in and gone along with any of Cardinal Essey's policies. There is definitely a cover up going on."

"Wow," exclaimed Jill. "This is getting scary. It's hard to know who's telling the truth."

"There's more," Jojo went on. "That very same night, the train my parents were supposedly on, crashed head on into another train; one that shouldn't have been on the track at that time. Everyone on board, all 200, was killed. It was one of the worst train wrecks in American history."

"That's so sad," said Jill, as her eyes began to well up with tears. "Jojo, I'm so sorry."

"Me, too," said Hooch, as Gus just shook his head in disbelief.

"And I thought being given up for adoption was bad," said Gus. "I'm really sorry, Jojo."

"Thanks," he said pausing briefly to collect himself. "What's really strange is that they found all of the bodies after the wreck, except for my mom and dad. To this day, their bodies have never been recovered."

"Everyone else was found?" asked Hooch.

"Yes," Jojo answered, "everyone, except my parents."

The Saints went quiet. No one talked for what seemed an eternity. If not for the whistle to end breakfast, and the screaming instructions from the Cafeteria Priest, they might still be there, sitting silently in disbelief.

"*Times up*!" yelled the Priest. "*Breakfast is over*! *We haven't got all day. Now bus your trays and get moving*!"

As the Saints got up to bus their trays, Jojo made one last comment.

"I think I know who has the answer to what *really* happened to my parents," he said as the excess food rolled off his tray into the garbage. "It's in the Cardinal's Sanctified Chambers, I know it!"

"Yeah, that's what it sounds like to me, too," said Hooch, as Jill nodded her head in agreement. "What do you say we sneak out tonight and have a look see?"

"Oh, I plan on it," said Jojo. "The next cleansing is…," started Jojo, as Hooch interrupted.

"Tonight!" he said. "And then your birthday is…"

"I know, I know," said Jojo. "Tomorrow night."

"Do you think the *It* will try to take you a day early, tonight at the cleansing?" asked Jill.

"Naw," said Jojo. "Thursday's are just for the oblivious general public. The Cardinal always likes to keep them in the dark. No, he keeps all internal cleansing private. Remember, these Underlings he has created, and is *continuing* to create here at the orphanage, are his special little fanatical followers. Why he's doing it, I'm not sure. How he's doing it is even more of a mystery. What I do know is that for some reason, the four of us are the only ones that seem to have any inkling as to what is going on; and it's up to us to try and stop it."

"Yeah, but how," asked Gus. "We're only a bunch of kids who are *real* close to becoming like the rest of them. What can we do?"

"Well," said Jojo, "the first thing is to be sure we *don't* become like the Underling's. And time is running out, which means we need to get out of here and get some answers. Are you with me?"

All of the Saints looked at each other, nodded their heads, and grinned. Hooch spoke for the group.

"Jojo," he said, "we're the 31st Street Saints, remember? And we *always* stick together!"

They all high-fived each other, as Hooch posed the most pressing question.

"When do we escape this rat hole?"

Jojo said firmly and clearly, "Tonight at 11:00 p.m. We'll meet at the automotive shed right across from the side entrance that leads to the secret passageway of the Cardinal's Sanctified Chambers. Keep your backpacks light. We'll need to be quick on our feet."

And with that Jill disappeared into the mass of girls filing up and away to their dorm rooms, as Jojo and the guys made their way up to Room 7.

No more was said as Hooch, Gus, and Jojo made their way back to their room to get ready for a day's work. It was a usual arduous Saturday, with clothes to be washed, floors to be scrubbed, and trash to be hauled just for starters. But, as ordinary and boring a Saturday as it may have appeared to other orphans, a very *unordinary* and *eventful* evening for the 31st Street Saints was about to occur.

All four kids knew that running away was risky business. No one in the history of the All Saints Orphanage had ever successfully escaped. Many had tried, but all were soon captured and returned. In order to make sure other inmates didn't get it in their heads to try and run, the punishment upon any runaway by the Priests was immediate and severe.

Though never mentioned to the public by the Information Priest, complete isolation for runaways was assured, in the Hole, when captured. The public would be given a watered down version of what the punishment would be, like making the kids do extra dish washing, scrubbing and peeling potatoes, or something of the like. Hooch and Jojo knew better. Having made brief visits to the Hole too many times before for *minor* offenses, both knew the dire consequences if caught as a runaway. And bread, water, and solitary confinement in the Hole for *many* days on end, was not something any of them looked forward to. They all knew getting caught was not an option.

The Saints finished their usual work routine, never letting on to anyone about the escape. None of the Priests were any the wiser that something *extraordinary* was about to take place on *this* particular Saturday.

"Now," whispered Jojo, as the Night Shift Priest called for lights out and quiet for the evening. "We must move quickly. Remember to pack lightly. Just the bare necessities like a toothbrush, change of clothes, and hooded sweatshirt. And…Hooch?"

"Yeah?"

"Clean underwear, too."

"Right," said Hooch, "*real* funny. Ha! Ha! Look at me. I can barely hold back the laughter."

"Hey," whispered Gus. "What about the twins?"

"Yeah," said Hooch. "We can't just leave them."

"We have to," said Jojo, looking over at Lou and Bob who were sound asleep. "It's too dangerous. Besides, we don't have enough bikes to handle everyone. They're still young enough not to have to worry about the *It*. We'll come back for them as soon as we can; most definitely before their thirteenth birthday."

Both Hooch and Gus felt awful about leaving them. They were like part of a family. But they knew Jojo was right. The twin's weren't strong enough for the adventure that was about to take place.

After packing and hiding their backpacks under their cots, they waited restlessly for bed check. As 9:00 p.m. came around, so did the Night Priest. He opened the door, made a quick head count, and then left as abruptly as he had entered.

The boys remained quiet, though, knowing that one more bed check for a final evening head count was coming at 10:30 p.m. by the notorious *It*. After that, the escape and the adventure for answers would begin.

The Escape

After what seemed an eternity, 10:30 p.m. finally arrived. The door slowly creaked open, as the *It* entered the room. The suffocating smell of liquor and onions permeated the room, as the *It* slowly and methodically maneuvered between the beds, carefully taking a head count counting along the way.

As if on cue, the *It* came to a stop at Jojo's bed. This was usual procedure for those orphans who were close to turning thirteen. "Soon, very soon," was mumbled, as a haunting laugh then emanated from within the hooded presence. Jojo's only thought was, *not tonight, you slime, not tonight.* The *It* then moved toward the door and opened it, pausing briefly before exiting the room. As the door creaked shut, the coast was clear. Jojo and the Saints hopped out of bed and headed for the window they would escape through, which was located at the south section of Room 7.

Quietly, he pulled up the shade revealing a window with many bars on it; bars put there to prevent any escape. He opened the window and carefully removed the two center bars that he and Hooch had spent many hours secretly loosening for this very moment. Once removed, there was just enough room for the Saints to squeeze through.

"Let's go," he whispered. "Hooch, you go first. Hand me your backpack and shinny down the rain gutter. It'll hold. I'm sure of it. I'll drop your backpack to you when you get down."

With that, Hooch maneuvered between the barred windows and began his descent. He needed to go first, as he was the strongest. If worst came to worst, though only twelve, he was much stronger than kid's years ahead of him and would be able to quiet any Underling that might be patrolling the grounds. Part of the dirty work of the Underlings was making sure no orphan was out and about after bed check. And they were very good at finding anyone who was.

In Hooch's case, it would be bad news for any Underling that *did* try to stop him. His major concern, though, was the *It*, who he hoped was making bed checks and not paying attention to what was going on outside.

When Hooch reached the ground, Jojo dropped him his backpack. He then turned to Gus and said, "You're next." Gus handed his backpack to Jojo, and climbed out of the window.

One lone gust of wind caused a rustling of the posters that hung on Room 7's walls. Outside the window, before beginning his descent, Gus glanced back in the direction of the room that had been his home these past years. *Good riddance*, was his one and only thought as he quickly climbed down the rain gutter.

Gus was the youngest of the Saints, and the most athletic. He could run, jump, hit, or do anything better than any of the inmates at the 31st Street Institution. He was at the bottom of the gutter before Jojo had one leg out the window.

After Gus had safely reached the ground, Jojo dropped down his and Gus' backpacks. He then climbed out the window, closed it behind him, and quickly shinnied down. Gus and Hooch greeted him from behind some bushes, as Jill, to everyone's pleasant surprise, suddenly arrived, as well.

"You made it!" said Hooch, giving Jill a hug. "Perfect timing. Any trouble?"

Hooch knew what the answer was going to be before he asked it. Jill was incredibly athletic. Sneaking out of a room and climbing down a rain gutter was no challenge for her at all.

"Nope," she said smiling. "Piece a cake. No one had a clue that I was leaving; I made sure of that. I'm so excited to leave this place. I wouldn't miss this adventure for anything; even if there is a chance we might end up in the Hole."

"That ain't gonna happen!" said Hooch, emphatically with a smile.

"All right, then, let's go!" said Jojo, as four shadowy figures streaked across the orphanage grounds to the automotive shed. Once there, the Saints gathered around Jojo, who began discussing the plan for entering the Sanctified Chambers.

"Now," started Jojo, "we'll leave our backpacks here. That way we'll be able to move quicker throughout the Cathedral. We'll enter at the side entrance, right there," he said pointing at a small dimly lit door some 100 yards away from them. "Jill and Hooch will remain outside on watch while…"

"Hey!" interrupted Hooch. "How come I can't go in?"

"Because there might be some Underling's patrolling around, and Jill will need your help," countered Jojo. "And, besides, I thought you'd love being…"

But before Jojo could finish his thought, lights and alarms from the orphanage dorms went off. From the Saints' Room 7 window, the shadowy hooded figure of the *It* leaned out and bellowed, "*Seize them*!!"

"Busted!" screamed Jojo. "To the bikes!"

Hooch grabbed a crow bar that he and Gus had hid near the door. He slid the bar under the lock. With one mighty thrust, the lock broke off and the door flew open. Hooch and Gus quickly made their way to two dirt bikes at the back of the shed.

One of the many talents of Hooch and Gus was that of being amazing mechanics, especially for kids so young. Early on the Priests had become aware of their talents and love of tinkering with automotive equipment. Whenever work needed to be done on the orphanage vehicles an elderly mechanic, who had taken both kids under his wing as apprentices, would ask the Priests for their help. Knowing what good work they did, the Priests consistently obliged.

As a reward for their help, the old mechanic let them work on a couple of old, broken down 120 Yamaha dirt bikes. In no time at all, they had the bikes in perfect working order. On days when all of the work was completed early, the old mechanic let Hooch and Gus ride throughout the many acres of the forest that surrounded the orphanage.

The two of them would ride for hours at a time. In a matter of weeks, they became expert bikers, able to jump creeks and fallen timber, climb steep hills, and basically go on any terrain and perform any maneuver they wanted. They knew every piece of ground for miles and miles deep into the forest.

The only place they were told never to ride was into the fenced off land where an old hermit named Mr. Cherub resided. His land bordered on the back or south side of the orphanage. It was also adjacent to the Tall-Tree Industries, a logging firm that owned the land on which the orphanage was built. Many believed that Mr. Cherub's land was haunted, and people who traveled out that way were uneasy about the mist that enveloped his 150 acre piece of land. It was local lore that whoever entered into the mist, stayed in the mist.

As legend would have it, the mist arrived at the same time Mr. Cherub did, over one hundred years ago, lingering as thick as pea soup. It didn't matter what the season was, winter, summer, spring, or fall—the mist never left.

A great oak tree, a tree of unearthly proportions, was situated at the center of the mist. It was immensely huge, and dwarfed the hundreds of gigantic firs that surrounded it. In the zero visibility created by the mist, the only visible part of the great oak was the middle section hundreds of feet up. The top of the oak disappeared into the clouds, invisible to the naked eye. By a special town ordinance, this great oak was given landmark status, and could never be cut down. Not even by Mr. Cherub himself.

It was on this land that the boys were told by the old mechanic never to ride. Both Hooch and Gus were warned that if they ever did mistakenly go onto old man Cherub's land, they were never to talk with him if he happened to cross their path.

"If you do by accident wander onto his land, run for your lives if you see him. No one's seen him for over a hundred years. He may even be dead, for all anyone knows. But

I don't think so. I think he's still alive, black magic or something. Don't take chances. If he is still alive, and I think he is, and he catches you, you'll never escape."

And then the old mechanic told them more.

He explained how Mr. Cherub and the mist arrived soon after the building of the Saint Barnabus the Munificent Cathedral was complete. Cardinal Essey, also a man of over one hundred years, was the first and only leader of the Cathedral. Church lore has it that *his* old age and great health were attributed to the grace of God, not black magic. From the very first Sunday Mass, which was the one and only church service Mr. Cherub attended, he and Cardinal Essey never got along.

Mr. Cherub's dislike and distrust of the Cardinal, and all of the Saint Barnabus Cathedral policies, were well documented. He called them dangerous and erroneous in every respect, quickly making him the most despised citizen in the town of Chewela. The majority of the townspeople worshipped the powerful Cardinal, and because Mr. Cherub didn't, he soon became thought of as a crazy old coot—a fanatic; an individual to avoid and shun. Mr.Cherub never returned again to the Cathedral, or the town. He grew all his own food and never left his supposedly haunted land.

To make matters worse, he also snubbed his nose at the all-powerful Tall-Tree Industries. They coveted his land for its wealth of majestic old growth Douglas Fir, including the great oak. Mr. Cherub vowed never to sell any of his trees on his 150 acres of land to Tall-Tree Industries, or anyone else, for that matter. He made this declaration at the one and only Chewela Town Meeting he ever attended. It was a clear, cool autumn evening that night, and the moon was full.

His speech was brief and concise. "I," he declared, leaning gently on his hickory cane, "will never sell."

After making his stance on never selling his land crystal clear, the people booed. He just smiled and left the building. Cardinal Essey, who led the town meetings, feeling angry and defeated, decided that one last try at convincing Mr. Cherub to sell was the will of the Lord. He sent two Priests after him.

"Quick," the old mechanic remembers the Cardinal telling the Priests. "Go and convince Mr. Cherub to return."

The two Priests raced out of the building Mr. Cherub had left only moments before. To their amazement, he was nowhere to be found. They checked around the outer part of the building and even up and down the streets and alleyways. Nothing—and he was never to be seen or heard of again. Both Hooch and Gus never forgot what the old mechanic had said.

"Hurry!" yelled Jojo. "Get the bikes going, and let's get out of here!!"

"*Get the runaways*!!" screamed the oncoming Underlings, as Hooch and Gus rolled their bikes out of the shed and climbed on. They flipped the engine on, and began cranking down hard to start the engine. The loud whirring and whining noise of the two souped-up motor bikes rang through the night.

"Climb on!" they shouted, as Jill jumped on behind Hooch and Jojo behind Gus. Screams could be heard from the Priests' quarters, as the Underlings drew closer shouting, "*Runaways*! *Get them*!"

"Go! Go!" shouted Jill.

She and Hooch sped off leading the way with Gus and Jojo close behind. As planned earlier, they headed in the only direction they figured the Underlings would not want to follow, south toward Mr. Cherub's haunted land. Hooch and Gus weren't too thrilled about it; but it was the only way.

"The cowards will never follow us into the mist," Jojo was heard to say as the four Saints sped away. Lights from bikes ridden by the Underlings lit up the night behind them.

"Don't slow down!" shouted Jojo to Gus. "They seem to be gaining on us!"

Gus just screamed out, "Don't worry! We're almost there!"

And with that he made an extreme right turn following close on Hooch's heels. Jojo held on tight, as he noticed a huge barb wired fence, maybe fifteen feet high, rapidly approaching.

"Gus! That looks like a fence coming up! A *tall* fence! Hey…Gus!" shouted Jojo, as Gus slowed down and pulled along side of Hooch and Jill. No words were spoken, as both drivers looked at each other and nodded.

"Hang on!" they yelled, as both Jojo and Jill did just that.

In the next split second, both engines were gunned to the maximum as they sped toward an enormous mound of dirt; first Hooch and Jill, with Gus and Jojo right behind. Up the mound of dirt they went, sailing over the barbed wire fence. The take off and flight through the air were perfect. The landing wasn't.

The bikes hit hard, skidding on their sides as they landed. All four Saints rolled and bounced across the ground. In front of them was the dreaded mist; behind they heard the Underlings approaching the mound of dirt leading over the fence.

"Is everyone all right?" yelled Jojo, as he picked himself up and made his way over to Gus who was checking his bike.

"Yeah, I'm fine," he answered. "But my bike is trashed."

"Mine, too," moaned Hooch, as he ran over to Jill and helped her off the ground. "Are you all right?"

"Yeah, I'll be fine," she said wiping off some dirt. "A couple bruises...nothing bad."

"How are you, Jojo?" asked Gus, shaking his head in disbelief. "Man...you just went *airborne* the second we landed. I thought we'd be picking up pieces of you all over the place."

"I'm fine," said Jojo, as he came limping slightly from a few yards away. "I twisted my ankle a bit, but I can walk."

"Well, you better be able to do better than walk," said Jill, as she pointed behind them, "'cause it looks like the Underlings aren't quite as frightened of Cherub's land as we had hoped."

It was at that point that the first of what was to be many bikes ridden by the Underlings sailed over the barbed wire fence toward them.

"Quick!" shouted Jojo, "into the mist!"

"The *what*?!" exclaimed Gus. "I'm not going in there. I know it was part of the plan, but I never thought the Underlings would really follow us this far. If we go in, we'll never get out! No way! I'll take my chances out here!"

"Fine, do what you want!" yelled Jojo. "*I'm* not getting caught!"

As the words left his mouth, the sound of bikes hitting the ground could be heard. Jojo took off running, limping slightly, toward the mist some twenty yards away.

"We're right behind you!" hollered Jill and Hooch, as Gus turned and made his way back to his bike.

"They're crazy to go in there," he mumbled to himself, picking his bike up off the ground. "It'll start, I know it will," he said, preparing to crank up the engine and get out of there.

But before even getting the chance to turn the engine over once, the first Underling to cross the fence tackled him, knocking him off his bike onto the ground.

"*I've got one*!" he shouted, and pinned Gus to the ground so he couldn't escape.

"Gus!" yelled Hooch, as he turned to go rescue his friend.

"No!" shouted Jill. "Hooch, there's too many of them. You'll be caught, too!"

"Gus!" he screamed again, as Jojo grabbed him by the arms.

"She's right, Hooch!" yelled Jojo. "We'll get him back; not now, but we *will* get him back. Now...we've *got* to go!"

"Quickly, they're almost here!" yelled Jill, as she began moving toward the mist.

"They'll pay for this," Hooch mumbled under his breath, looking back one last time at his good friend before following after Jojo and Jill, "*big* time."

"*Get the others*!" shouted what had to be the leader, as three Underlings ran toward them. They were too late, though, as Jojo, Jill and Hooch disappeared into the mist.

"*Follow them*!" shouted the lead Underling, but none of them moved.

"*Cowards*!!" he yelled again, striking one of the disobeying Underlings across the face.

He wheeled around and motioned for the other underlings to mount their bikes and leave.

"*They've escaped for the moment*!" he bellowed to no one in particular. "*They'll be ours soon enough*!"

"*Tie up the captured Saint, and put him behind my bike*!" ordered the leader.

And with that, the Underling gang sped away, as three figures moved with exceeding caution, deeper into the forbidden mist.

Into the Mist

"Hey, Jill…Jojo?!" yelled Hooch. "I can't see a thing! Where are you guys?!"

"We're right here," she said, grabbing him by the arm, causing him to jump a foot off the ground. "And quit making so much noise!"

"Don't do that!" Hooch yelled. "You know how I hate being surprised like that."

"Sorry, sorry," Jill said apologetically. "Now, we've got to be quieter."

"Yeah," whispered Jojo. "We don't know if the Underlings followed us or not."

"All right, all right," Hooch whispered back shaking his head in disbelief at what had happened to Gus. "I just can't believe that we left Gus behind. How did that happen? We're supposed to stick together."

"Look," said Jill. "I'm as upset about Gus as you are. He *is* my brother, *remember*? I'm sick about it, but there was nothing we could do. There was *no way* he was going to follow us."

"He made a bad choice, Hooch," said Jojo. "He was bound and determined to stay out of the mist."

"Okay, okay," Hooch sighed dejectedly. "But some way or another, we've got to get him back."

"We will," said Jojo, as he urged both Hooch and Jill to focus back on the situation at hand.

"Now," he continued, "let's move deeper into the mist and lay quiet for awhile. If the Underlings did follow, and we remain quiet, they'll for sure get frustrated and give up. Then we can backtrack our way out."

"Sounds good to me," said Jill, as something nearby grabbed at her leg.

"Nice try, Hooch," she said. "But I don't scare as easily as you do."

"Nice try?" questioned Hooch. "What are you talking about?"

"You mean...you didn't just grab my leg?" she asked, as a shudder ran down her spine.

"Ah...*no*, and...are you messing with me again?" asked Hooch, as something grabbed his leg, as well.

"*Yeeooww*!" he screamed. "Jill! Something grabbed my leg, too!"

"*Jojo*!" they both yelled in unison. "Was that *you*?"

"No, I didn't grab either of you. And quit yelling! You'll lead the Underlings right..." But before he could finish, he too let out a scream.

"Hey!" he yelled, pulling both Hooch and Jill closer to him. "What *was* that?"

The three of them froze, not speaking a word, fearful that it might be one of the Underling's toying with them before pouncing.

"Jojo…what do we do? What *do* we *do*?" Hooch whispered, as the answer came, but it wasn't Jojo. And it wasn't an Underling, either.

"What *do* we *do*?
What *do* we *do*?
Oh, how silly are—
The three of you!
The three of you!"

"Who's there?!" shouted Hooch, in his most menacing voice. "Show yourself!"

"Hooch, Hooch
Oh, so strong,
I've been here with you
All along—
All along."

"Stop that!" Hooch yelled again.

"Yes," added both Jojo and Jill. "And who *are* you?"

"I am a friend
A friend of you three,
Follow my voice—
And you will see
And you will see."

"Hey, Jojo?!" yelled Hooch. "Do you think it might be an Underling?'

But before Jojo could answer, the voice did.

"Underlings, Underlings
No worry for them,
They've fled the great mist
Never to return again—
Never to return again."

After a brief silence Jill said, "We don't have a whole lot of options here, do we? And whatever it is, I sense a kindness about it. We've got nothing to lose. I choose we follow."

"Oh, yeah, right," questioned Hooch. "Let's follow this rhyming *idiot* off to who knows where and…"

Jojo cut in.

"I agree with Jill," said Jojo.

Hooch just moaned and muttered, "Figures," under his breath, as the voice spoke again.

"An idiot me?
Oh, we shall see—
Hooch, listen to them
It is the right choice,
Follow my voice,
Follow my voice."

"This way," said Jojo, as Jill grabbed onto Hooch, stumbling ever so slightly.

"Sorry, Hooch," she said, as he suddenly stopped abruptly in his tracks.

"Why are you stopping?" she asked.

"Shhhhhh!" he said, as Jill's grip on his arm tightened. "I've lost hold of Jojo, and I can barely hear the voice. Hey…Jojo? Jojo, where are you?"

"I'm over here!" he yelled. "Over here, this way!"

"All right, Hooch, let's keep moving," encouraged Jill, as she pushed him off in the direction of Jojo's voice.

"I am…I am!" he shouted. "Just stop pushing. I don't want to trip into a hole or…"

But before he could finish his thought, a thunderous scream off in the distance, filled the air.

"*Eeeooowww*!!" went the scream, and then silence.

"Hooch!" yelled Jill. "Hooch, did you hear that? It was Jojo, I'm sure of it. And it came from just a few yards away."

In her zeal, Jill now took the lead. "Come on!"

"Fine…Fine!" yelled Hooch, grasping at Jill's arm as she ran forward. "Just stay with me!"

Another loud noise was heard, causing Jill to bolt in that direction. Hooch lost his grip on her arm.

"Jill! Hey, Jill! Slow down. Come back here!" he shouted. "Where are you?!"

"I'm over here. Come straight toward my voice. There's a huge tree in front of me, that….." But before she could finish her thought, a piercing scream, similar to Jojo's was heard.

"*Eeeooowww*!!" and then as before, there was silence, a deafening silence.

Hooch found himself all alone. "Guys…uh….guys…is anybody there?" he said, as he made his way cautiously in the direction he last heard Jill's voice.

"Owwwww!" he said, bumping his head into the trunk of a tree, a really *big* tree.

"Ahhhhh, this must be the tree that Jill was…"

And then, as with the others, another loud scream was

let out. Only this time, it was from Hooch. "*Eeeooowww*!!" he screamed; and then again there was silence.

New Friends

After what seemed the longest of all free falls imaginable, into sheer darkness, Jill landed with a thud, right on top of Jojo.

"Owwwww!" he yelled, as she thanked him for breaking her fall. But, before he could get her off of him, Hooch joined in the festivities.

"Owwwww!!" they shouted in unison, as Hooch landed squarely on top of them. "Get off! You're crushing us!" Hooch just rolled off, laughing.

"*Whhhoooeee*!" he exclaimed. "Let's do that again!"

"Yeah…right," mumbled Jojo, who was not amused at all. "Except this time *I'll* go last."

"Oh, quit whining," said Hooch. "At least we're all back together again. And, man, oh man, was that first step a *doozie*, or what?"

"Yeah," added Jill. "First I was hugging a tree, and then—bam—I'm in a free fall. Crazy!"

"Okay, okay," said Jojo, "chill out, would you, guys? I'm

glad you're having so much fun, but we really need to figure out how to get out of here, wherever *here* is. Any ideas?"

The exhilaration they all felt from the free fall turned somber in a hurry, as the impact of their new surroundings took hold.

Torches on the walls of what appeared to be a meticulously dug tunnel cast ghostly shadows everywhere, giving the Saints the creeps. No one spoke, as the only sound besides their breathing was the drips of moisture falling on the tunnel floor. The silence was broken, but not in the way any of the Saints would ever have expected.

"It's so nice of you to drop in," a pleasant high-pitched voice was heard to say. "We've been expecting you."

All three kids spun in the direction of the voice, not knowing who or what had just spoken. "Where are you?" demanded Jojo. "Show yourself!"

"I'm right here," the voice said again. "One more step back, and you'll be standing on top of me."

"Whoa!" exclaimed Jill. "Do you see what I see?" she asked, as the kids found themselves staring at a mouse. And not just any mouse.

"Uh-huh," mumbled Hooch. "And it talks."

"Of course, I talk," he answered back. "My name is Whitsnit, head servant of the caretaker of Mid-Heaven, Master Cherub."

"No way!" said Hooch. "You mean the same Cherub that the mechanic back at the orphanage told us to avoid, *at all costs*? *That* Cherub?"

"That would be, Master Cherub, to you," Whitsnit replied. "And, yes, they are one and the same. It is a pleasure to meet the 31st Street Saints."

Whitsnit then slowly removed his top-hat, adjusted his spectacles, and switched his cane from right hand to left in preparation for what turned out to be a very grand bow.

Upon rising slowly after bowing for a socially acceptable amount of time, he added, "As I mentioned before, we've been expecting you, and we're glad you've arrived."

"He is so cute," whispered Jill, doing everything possible not to giggle.

But Hooch was having none of that. "How come you've stopped speaking in that annoying rhyming voice of yours?" asked Hooch.

"Ah, yes," continued Whitsnit. "The annoying rhymes. That would be my servant, Quidley, you're referring to. That's him coming this way, as we speak."

It was at that moment that a very large, round bellied, four foot tall whistling mole stepped out of the shadows to greet them. He appeared a rather jolly fellow, and around his midriff hung a carpenter's belt with every digging tool imaginable. On his head he wore a very dirty duster, backwards, giving him the appearance of a portly, yet very colorful, jockey.

Upon seeing the Saints, he stopped his whistling, and tried as best he could to bow, though his belly and tools made any sort of movement towards his feet a very difficult endeavor, indeed.

"Yes, yes, the rhymer is me
The rhymer is me you see,
Quite annoying to you—
So, *very* annoying to you,
Yet, quite effective for me."

"Oh, sorry about that, my boyfriend didn't really mean it," apologized Jill, who was still holding back her laughter as best she could. "You're not annoying at all."

"Oh, yes he is!" exclaimed Hooch. "You're an *extremely* annoying little runt, you know that porky?"

Quidley, taking offense to the comment grabbed a hold of a hand-sized trowel, and moved toward Hooch in a confrontational manner. Whitsnit quickly moved between them. Jojo stepped in as well.

"You'll have to excuse my friend," Jojo said. "He can be a bit gruff at times."

Hooch glared at Jojo, but said nothing.

"Yes, Quids," said the little mouse. "We must remember, they are topside dwellers and know no better. Now, shouldn't you be off to do more digging for Master Cherub?"

"Ah, yes, Master Mouse, Master Mouse
I hear you loud and clear,
It's off for me to busy be
Must now be gone from here—
Must now be gone from here."

And with another brief attempt to bow, a stern glance in Hooch's direction, Quidley spun on his heels, commenced whistling a hearty tune, and waddled away out of sight. The clanging sound of his tool belt faded in the distance.

"Hey, thanks, Whitnut," said Hooch. "I appreciate you straightening out your friend like that. For such a little guy, you've got spunk. You remind me a little bit of Whiskers, a pet mouse at one of the foster homes I used to live."

Hooch bent over to pet Whitsnit, but the mouse would

have nothing of it. A quick crack on his finger by his cane caused him to draw quickly aback.

"Owwwww!" shouted Hooch. "That hurt!"

"You deserved it!" countered the mouse. "And the name's *Whitsnit*! Not, *Whitnut*!"

The authority with which the little mouse spoke took the Saints by surprise.

"And I am *not* Whisker's," he continued, "and definitely not *anybody's* pet!"

"All right, all right, enough already!" said Jojo quickly intervening, as Hooch mumbled something about a psycho rodent while massaging his bruised finger and ego.

"Now," continued Jojo, "you said *we* were expecting you? Where are the others?"

"Why," began Whitsnit, gathering his composure once again, "they will be here, momentarily."

Jill, feeling the need to explore a bit before the 'others' arrived, took a step forward only to be cautioned against moving any further.

"I wouldn't take another step," he said. "That's a bottomless shaft you're moving towards. And besides, I believe the, *we,* you were asking about have arrived."

Jill couldn't help herself, though, and inched a bit closer. "I can't see any..." she began

as out of nowhere a whoosh of air exploded up the shaft producing what looked to be a flying carpet of fur—hundreds of intertwined squirrels, chattering away incessantly, in nattily attired aviator gear consisting of gloves, goggles, and helmets. The carpet hovered in the middle of the shaft with uncanny precision.

"Bushtail!" shouted Whitsnit with a smile, "so good to see you!"

"Likewise, 'cuz, climb aboard!" shouted what had to be the lead squirrel, who gave a quick salute back to Whitsnit. "Your friends, too, if they like!"

"Captain Bushtail," said Whitsnit, "I'd like to introduce you to the 31st Street Saints."

The Ride

"It's a pleasure to meet you!" shouted Captain Bushtail. "Please, climb aboard!"

The three Saints looked first at each other, then the flying-carpet, then at each other again. "This just gets crazier by the minute," was all Jojo could muster. "Well, what do you think?"

After a brief moment of silence, Hooch exclaimed, "I sure don't want to stay in this black hole any longer. Let's do it!"

"That's the spirit!" yelled Whitsnit, who was already aboard and secured at the front.

"Now step lively. Time is a wasting!"

As Jill moved forward to board first, Captain Bushtail warned, "Now, watch that first step."

"Not a problem," she said trying to appear calm, while teetering ever so slightly onto the carpet. Hooch and Jojo followed quickly behind, grabbing on tightly, albeit, it seemed a bit *too* tight.

"Ouch!" yelled out one of the squirrels, in Hooch's direction. "A little higher, if you please."

"Oh...yeah...gotcha," replied a blushing Hooch. "Sorry about that."

"No problem!" the squirrel yelled back. "Happens all the time!"

And with that, the command to depart was given. Like a bullet, the flying carpet shot up through a hollow section of the immense trunk of the Great Oak at breakneck speed, with the Saint's eyes squinting and holding on for dear life. In an effort to miss an immense knot in the tree, the carpet swung violently sideways causing Jill to lose her grip. For a brief moment, it appeared that she might roll off the carpet and into the bottomless shaft.

"Jill!" screamed out Hooch, as he made a move to grab her.

But a quick command by the Captain took care of that. "*Adjust*!" he hollered.

With precision timing and teamwork, the entire carpet knew exactly what to do. In the blink of an eye, the section she was on lowered itself ever so slightly, cradling her securely like a baby. Jill was out of danger.

"*Good call, Cap*!" yelled out the carpet in unison.

"I should say so!" laughed Jill. Her confidence in the carpet, as did everyone else's, instantly skyrocketed. All of the Saints were then able to relax, settle back, and enjoy the ride of their life.

Like sailors getting use to the sway of the sea, the Saints learned quickly to adjust to the quick deft maneuvers of the carpet. Crooks and bends in the tree flew by, ever upward, as the Saints leaned and moved accordingly. After what seemed an hour or so, a sliver of light could be seen up ahead.

"Steady now, boys!" shouted Bushtail. . "One more quick left, and we'll be home free!"

All of the squirrels responded with an, "Aye, aye, Cap'!"

On Bushtail's command, all squirrels directed their tails in rudder-like fashion causing the carpet to cut sharply to the left shooting out the top of the tree into an open air expanse. Then, with the skill of a professional aviator, Captain Bushtail directed the carpet to an immediate stop, where it hovered over an enormous stone and wooden structure. This structure, as they lowered closer, was an amazing sight. It was a mansion floating in the clouds.

"It's huge!" exclaimed Jojo. "I've never seen anything like it!"

A gust of wind caused the carpet to drift through some smoke arising out of an enormous stone chimney. The Saints wiped a strand of smoke away from their faces as it curled its way up and out of the chimney.

"Sorry about that!" shouted Bushtail. "Master Cherub has his fire burning a bit early, today."

He then directed the carpet out of the smoke and into a slow, steady descent to a large deck area below. It hovered some two feet above the deck, just high enough for the Saints and Whitsnit to slide off with ease. After a flight like that, the solid deck felt good.

"Ah, yes," said a smiling Hooch, stomping his feet on the deck. "Now, *that's* what I'm talking about!"

"Yeah," added Jojo. "Thanks for the joy ride boys, but it sure feel's good to be standing on something other than air."

The carpet said their good-byes, and in a blink of an eye disbanded into hundreds of separate flying squirrels that disappeared into the cloud on which the mansion now rested.

All departed but Bushtail, who stood straight and erect on the deck railing.

"Thanks for permitting us to help you in your time of need," he said removing his goggles off his nose and onto his forehead. "We're here to serve if the need arises again."

And with that, he pulled his goggles back down, gave a slight bow, back-flipped off the deck into a barrel roll, and disappeared into the clouds below.

"Show-off," mumbled Whitsnit, as the mansion's huge wooden door, set in a stone frame, began to open.

All eyes turned to see who was there. The door creaked to a halt, exposing what had to be the Master Cherub that Whitsnit so often referred to.

"Greetings!" hailed a short but stocky built fellow. He proceeded towards them in a long flowing white robe, giving the appearance that he was gliding on air. A marvelously crafted crooked staff was clutched in his right hand. "I see from your tousled hair and watery eyes, that the trip on our flying carpet of furry friends was a swift and drafty one!"

His smile glistened in the sunshine, with piecing blue eyes that seemed to see right through you. His entire face was aglow, beaming out from amongst a thick white speckled beard that hung almost the length of his robe.

"My name is Master Cherub, keeper of this place called, Mid-Heaven. Welcome to my home!" he said, as he gave an open palmed sweeping gesture in front of him displaying his land down below. Rolling hills, lush valleys, pristine lakes and rivers beneath a brilliant blue sky, paraded before them as far as the eye could see.

"It's a pleasure to meet you!" chimed in the Saints, still somewhat in awe of all that had taken place.

"This place is amazing!" exclaimed Hooch, as he stared out over the vast expanse down below. "What are those little dots all over the place?"

"If you are referring to the 'dots' with smoke coming out of them, they are the homes of this land, where the faithful servants of King Mai the Omni reside," he said. "They are the special few who stayed true to the King and His Son, Lord Nos, and were not deceived during the Great Fall."

"But enough questions for now," said Master Cherub. "Let me get you some food and drink, as it's been too long since you've last supped."

With that he directed them into his home. The door opened without any assistance, and closed behind them once inside, in the same manner. The Saints followed the flowing robe of Master Cherub down a long corridor beneath a curved archway that led into a huge banqueting hall. A table with masterfully crafted high backed oak chairs, arrayed with exquisite silver table settings, was adorned regally before them. Golden plates, filled with meats and cheeses of every kind, and goblets filled to the brim with juices were set ready for the taking.

"Please be seated," said Master Cherub. "Let us bow our heads and give thanks to our Great King Mai and His Son, Lord Nos, for all the mercy and grace they've bestowed upon us."

All of the Saints bowed their heads as Master Cherub gave thanks. Upon completion of his gracious prayer, a thunderous "A*men*!" roared forth.

"I'm starving!" exclaimed Jill, as a flurry of knives, forks, and goblets danced around the table. "I didn't know I was this hungry."

"Me, either!" piped in Hooch, in between gulps of food and juice. "Hey, Jojo, easy on the sausage; you know that stuff gives you gas!"

"Ha! The sausage is fine. It's *you* that gives me gas!" retorted Jojo, as laughter filled the room.

Everyone joyfully feasted, stopping only briefly for air, before indulging again. It was at one of those brief intervals between chewing and breathing that Jojo asked a question.

"Where did the people of Mid-Heaven come from? I didn't even know a place like this existed."

Master Cherub dabbed at his beard with a napkin. The Saints waited for him to finish one last bite before answering. After a slow sip of juice, and another quick dab, he cleared his throat and spoke.

"The people you see in the land below are the survivors of the Great War. They are those that remained true to King Mai and His son, Lord Nos. I, too, am one of the survivors; now head servant of the King and Lord, and the caretaker of this land and these people."

"What war? I don't remember reading about any Great War, or King Mai, or Lord Nos," asked Jill. "Who took part in this war, anyways?"

"Yeah," said Hooch, "and why are *we* here? We had nothing to do with the war."

"And where, exactly, *is* here?" questioned Jojo.

"All in good time, all in good time," said Master Cherub, ever so calmly. "Let's move into the ante-chamber for some tea and mints." He motioned them towards the rear of the banqueting room. "A comfortable chair near the fire, before the journey that will answer all of your questions, will be just the thing."

"Journey?" asked Jojo, looking over at both Jill and Hooch in a curious way.

"You mean," asked Hooch looking around at all that was before them, "there's more?"

"Can't we get answers to our questions here?" asked Jill.

"All in good time," Master Cherub repeated, as he led them down a great hall into a room with a cobblestone floor, covered with plush rugs and huge cushioned high back chairs. The chairs encircled a massive stone fireplace. The blaze from the fire warmed them as they each found and snuggled into the chair of their choosing. After settling in nicly, Master Cherub gave a tap of his staff, one tap only, as Whitsnit appeared as if from nowhere with his top hat and cane in hand.

"Yes, Master?" asked Whitsnit, as he removed his hat with one of his glove covered paws. "May I be of service?"

"Ah, Whitsnit," smiled Cherub, "so good of you to come so promptly. It would be of great joy to me if you would bring our friends here some of our best tea and our sweetest, most succulent mints, for their pleasure. Would you be so kind?"

"As you wish, Master," he said bowing slightly.

With that, he turned away, donned his top hat, secured it snug on his head with a quick tap of his cane, and then disappeared from sight, all to the amazement and delight of the Saints.

"How does he do that?" asked Jill. "That is so cute!"

"Yeah," started Hooch, still simmering from the whack on his finger, "real cute. Now, what about this journey…" But before he could finish his thought, Whitsnit appeared, once again, out of nowhere. Only this time, he wasn't alone.

"Look sharp, now," ordered what looked to be the largest raccoon the Saints had ever seen. He was walking upright with a large silver platter on his shoulder. A steaming pewter teapot was centered perfectly on the platter surrounded by mints of every kind. Behind him appeared four smaller raccoons, also dressed in their white servant's attire, each with a teacup and saucer in hand. Single file and in perfect step, they marched over to the Saints and handed them each a cup. Whitsnit watched with smiling approval.

"I've said it before, and I'll say it again," said Jill. "This just keeps getting better!"

"Thank you," said the Saints, as they were handed their tea cup and some mints by the first three raccoons. The fourth, and tiniest of the raccoons, a female named Haras, made her way over to Master Cherub. It was she who had been the high privilege of serving her master.

"Thank you, Haras," said Cherub, as she curtsied, blushing ever so slightly. "And thanks and blessings to you, Sarge, and the other Servants of the House."

Sarge bowed lowly and graciously, said a quick, "Step lively, now!" then led his troops single file and in perfect unison past Whitsnit and out of the antechamber. As they passed by Whitsnit, they each gave a respectful bow and salute. Whitsnit returned their salutation with a nod and a smile and then turned to Master Cherub.

"If that is all, Master, I will be on my way," he said, bowing slightly, with top hat in hand.

"Please, Whitsnit," said Master Cherub. "Notify us when transportation for the journey has arrived."

"As you wish, Master," he replied, quickly donning his top hat, and then gracefully exiting the room.

"Is he always that obliging?" asked Jill. "That's a good little guy to have around, if you ask me."

"He is," answered Master Cherub. "And he is not only obliging, but is the Head Keeper of my house, and my most trusted and loyal friend."

After what could have been only minutes and barely enough time for the Saints to polish off the scrumptious mints and tea, Whitsnit returned.

"It's time, Master," he said, motioning toward French Doors that opened onto a balcony overlooking the landscape below, where perched on the balcony, was a Dove.

The Journey

The Saints moved closer to the doors trying to catch a glimpse of the Dove that Whitsnit was motioning to. It was beautiful, glistening in the Mid-Heaven sunlight.

"It's just a bird!" shouted Hooch, wondering what all of the fuss was about.

"But a beautiful one at that," said Jill, who found it difficult to take her eyes off of it.

"I take it," said Jojo, "that this isn't just *any* bird, right?" They all looked at Master Cherub and Whitsnit who had bent down on one knee, with heads bowed in reverence to the Dove.

"That would be correct," was the reply. But it wasn't from Whitsnit or Master Cherub, who remained silent and motionless on their knees. It came from the Dove.

"Whoa!" said Hooch, a bit startled at first. Then remembering where he was and what he had seen of this magical place already, he quickly added, "And why, I ask you all, should this be a surprise to any of us?"

"Ahhhhh, a son of earth in whom there is no guile!" said the Dove, who turned his gaze from Hooch toward Master Cherub and Whitsnit who were still on bended knee. "Please rise, oh servants of the Eno!" he gently commanded, as Master Cherub and Whitsnit rose to their feet, "and introduce me to our guests."

"Yes, my Prince," said Master Cherub, rising humbly to his feet.

"Prince?" questioned the Saints, not knowing whom Master Cherub was referring to.

"Please, Prince Tirips," Master Cherub said, motioning with his hand in the direction of the Saints. "I'd like to introduce you to the, 31st Street Saints of Earth."

Jill gave her best attempt at a curtsey, while the other Saints followed her lead and bowed slowly at the waist. As they rose up, the Dove was gone! Something most extraordinary had taken His place.

"Hey!" exclaimed Hooch, stepping backwards in terror at what had instantly appeared before them. "It's a giant! Where did he come from? Quick, run for your lives!"

"Giant?!" yelled Jojo, as he found himself staring at something entirely different, indeed. "That's no giant! That's a fierce warrior I see, with sword, a breastplate of brass, spear, and helmet. Back away, everyone! Back! And be quick about it!"

"Huh?" grunted Hooch, looking at Jojo in disbelief. "A warrior?" he asked again, rubbing his eyes and then gazing again on not a warrior, but instead, the very same giant he had just been looking at.

"Oh," called out Jill, quite sure that both of the boys were making fun of her. "How dare you speak in so vile a manner about someone so beautiful! That's not funny in the least! And listen to her singing. Can you hear it? It's so beautiful it makes me want to cry!" Her eyes began to well up with tears.

Hooch and Jojo turned and stared at Jill in disbelief. Then they looked at each other in wonder. "Beautiful?" questioned Hooch scratching his head, still thinking that they should all be running for their lives.

"Singing?" asked Jojo, more concerned with how they were going to defend themselves from such a ferocious warrior then with the singing that Jill thought she heard.

"Is there a problem?" asked Master Cherub, as the Saints turned around toward him.

"Yes, yes, there is!" exclaimed Jojo. "Why is it we each see something different in place of the Dove? What sort of trick is this?"

"And, by the way," asked Hooch, "where *is* the Dove?"

"Please forgive my brief exhibition," said Prince Tirips, as the Saints quickly turned back around to see, once again, the Dove.

"Hey!" shouted the Saints, as the beautiful woman, giant, and warrior had vanished from sight.

"As I was saying," replied the Prince making all in the room tremble ever so slightly, "forgive me. This was a lesson, though, that needed to be taught." The Dove then went on to explain that He takes many shapes and forms, depending on the occasion and need. The Saints were listening. "It is my hope that this small lesson will be one of many to come," said the Dove, nodding in the direction of Master Cherub and Whitsnit.

The two of them nodded back, and began making their way to the door. No words were spoken, but it was clear all the same that a message was given and understood.

"I am the third part of the Eno," said the Dove. "We, the Eno, are the body of three that rule and have ruled all of creation from the time before time. I am the Messenger and Guide, sent to you from Lord Nos, son of King Mai the Omni." After speaking, He flew from the window over to the door that Master Cherub and Whitsnit were heading towards.

"It is the hope and wish of Lord Nos and King Mai," continued the Dove, "that you, the 31st Street Saints, would accompany me and Master Cherub to meet the King and His Son at this time. It is in Their presence that all of your questions will be addressed."

The Saints were so engrossed in the words spoken by Prince Tirips that they were totally unaware they had been moving in the direction of the door, along with Master Cherub and Whitsnit. They found themselves standing outside the palatial mansion on Master Cherub's enormous multileveled deck. For the past few moments, the Saints had been content not to speak, intent on listening, instead. But that changed as Jojo found the Prince's request for them to go meet the King and His Son very intriguing.

"First of all," started Jojo, "it's not like we've had a whole lot of choice as to what has happened to us in the last twenty-four hours or so, have we? Events all along the way have happened completely out of our control, wouldn't you agree?"

"Yeah," added Hooch. "We didn't ask to fall down a hole in a tree, get a ride on a flying fur carpet, and every other weird thing that's happened, now did we? And now, you're *asking* us if we want to continue? What's up with the sudden change? Why not just make us? Why do we all of a sudden have a choice?"

The Dove said nothing. Master Cherub and Whitsnit said nothing. It was Jill that spoke next. "No," she said, looking down at the floor, shuffling one foot gently from side to side in a pensive manner. "I don't believe everything has been out of our choosing, especially one very important decision which started this adventure in the first place."

"And what was that?" asked Hooch, a bit annoyed that anyone, especially his girlfriend, would disagree with him.

"I'd like to hear this, as well," said Jojo.

Jill paused for a moment to gather her thoughts; then she began. "If my memory serves me correctly," she said, "we all agreed at breakfast one morning that we needed to find out some answers." She then went on to remind Jojo and Hooch, about everyone's concern over Jojo's upcoming birthday, and the awful consequences that came with that. She mentioned how, on top of that, everyone wanted to find the answer to the disappearance of Jojo's parents, as now also, the whereabouts of her brother, Gus. "All of this led to our agreeing to escape that night. No one twisted our arms or forced us to go. We did it, each of us, because we wanted to; we *needed* to, remember?"

Jojo and Hooch both just looked humbly at the floor, as Jill had, and began shuffling *their* feet, ever so slightly, back and forth. She was driving home some harsh realities that they had forgotten.

"She's right, Jojo," said Hooch. "We didn't want to lose you, and we wanted some answers, *lots* of answers. Everything Jill said is right. We couldn't wait to escape, and would have been caught, once we did, if Master Cherub and his Mid-Heaven helpers hadn't assisted us. Yep…we've made *all* our own choices *all* along the way."

Jojo nodded his head in agreement and blurted out, "How I could have forgotten all of this is beyond me! But this I now know. We escaped to find answers. And that's what we still need to do. We've come this far, and I don't know about the rest of you, but as for me, *I—we—*need to finish this; not only for my parent's sake, but for Gus as well. I just hope that we're not too late."

In the powerful yet peaceful voice of the Dove, came the reply, "You have decided wisely." The Dove continued. "There is always hope in the Eno, Jojo. Remember that. Now, we must be off. Time is of the essence, and the King and his Son are awaiting your arrival."

As the Dove finished speaking, something inconceivably wonderful happened. Before their very eyes, Prince Tirips the Dove, began to grow and grow and grow, until He was so immense that He became large enough to transport all of Saints and Master Cherub on His back, with room to spare.

"Climb aboard!" commanded the Dove, as the Saints eagerly did just that. Once settled onto Prince Tirips downy soft back, Whitsnit gave a whistle, as if calling for assistance; much more than that appeared before them.

"Look at that!" yelled Hooch. "What is it?"

All eyes instantly saw what Hooch had seen with jaw-dropping awe. From beneath the mansion, up through the clouds, appeared a massive, terrifying eagle like creature, with boulder crushing claws, twenty-foot wingspan, and many eyes circling its head. It flew up and hovered at the edge of the deck before them.

Riding the beast was a powerful looking warrior. Though seated on the beast, it was quite obvious that he had to be seven, maybe eight feet tall. He was similar in appearance to that of men of earth, but more, with granite-like arms and a chiseled chest, with a golden sash around his midriff. Leathery knee length boots protected powerful legs of steel. Mighty hands held the reins of the beast in one hand and a spear the size of a weaver's beam in the other. As he spoke, his flowing hair, golden like the sun, streamed behind him, held only in check by a glistening headband of shimmering gold.

"Wow!" was all that was heard from the quivering voices of the Saints.

They were simultaneously in awe of his presence and extremely thankful that they were nestled securely and safely aboard the Dove. This immense individual hovering on the mighty beast before them gave a military salute and a bow of reverance towards Prince Tirips. The Dove gave a courteous and respectful nod in return.

"Hello and good day to you, Kebatha, Captain of the Woe-Bird Cavalry of the High Heavens!" said Prince Tirips. "I see Keba, your trusty steed, looks healthy and ready for action!"

Upon hearing its name, the Woe-bird threw back its head in delight, exposing a powerful beak. It then emitted the terrifying, shrill battle cry of the Woe-Bird that strikes fear into all those that oppose the Eno. Both rider and Woe-Bird bowed respectfully, once again.

"It's so good to see you again, my Prince!" said Kebatha, "Master Cherub and faithful Whitsnit, as well!"

Master Cherub, Whitsnit, and Captain Kebatha all gave each other mutual nods of respect. Kebatha rested his spear across his lap, and glanced over at the Saints. "Are these son's and a daughter of man I see clinging to you? The fortunate guests I will be escorting to the Celestial City of Mansoul?"

"They are," stated the Dove, giving the children a look indicating it was all right for them to speak.

"It's a pleasure to meet you, sir," said the Saints in unison.

"Ah! I like them already!" shouted Kebatha, as he turned Keba toward the heavens.

"Enough talk, for now, though," he continued. "Commander Leachim, Commander of all the armies of the Eno, gave me strict orders to get you to the Celestial City of Mansoul by this evening. By your leave, my Prince, we must make haste!"

"Agreed!" answered Prince Tirips.

With that, Kebatha gave the command, "*On Keba*!" The mighty Woe-Bird faithfully complied by streaking skyward toward their destination. Prince Tirips, awaiting Master Cherub, was eager to depart, as well

"Shall we?" He said to Master Cherub, who was taking a brief moment to consult with Whitsnit.

He whispered some last words to his devoted friend and servant before setting him safely on the deck railing; then gracefully, he climbed onto the Dove. With all passengers safely aboard, and with Master Cherub making sure that the Saints were secure, the Dove announced preparation for takeoff.

"Hold on tight!" yelled Master Cherub, as Prince Tirips rocketed forward.

Soaring skyward toward the Celestial City of Mansoul, the land of Mid-Heaven whizzed by below them. The sight of the peaceful homes of the land quickly became a distant blur on the horizon. In the blink of an eye, the Dove and His passengers jettisoned forward catching up to their escort, Captain Kebatha.

"Enjoying the ride?" the Captain called out to the Saints, as he maneuvered alongside for a chat.

"Whoooeee!!" shouted Jojo from the front, with his hands tightly grasping the neck feathers of the Dove. "You better believe it! This is amazing!"

Jill held on tightly to Jojo's waist, and Hooch put his hands above his head as if on a roller-coaster at some Theme Park.

"Yeeeehaaaaww!" hollered Hooch, "if the kids at the orphanage could see me now!"

Captain Kebatha threw back his head and howled with laughter.

"This is just the beginning, my young friends. You are in for the adventure of your lives!"

And with that, he urged Keba forward into the lead, cutting the wind in front of Prince Tirips to make for a smoother flight. Master Cherub let out a chuckle of his own; the sight of the three joyful passengers brought a smile to his face.

"Careful, now!" he called out to Hooch, as a heavy air current slammed across his hands causing him to briefly lose his balance.

"Whoa!" exclaimed Hooch, quickly bringing down his hands, and clutching tightly to the Dove. "Gotcha, Boss!"

After a brief time the rushing of the wind and the steady, smooth cadence of the Dove's wings propelling them forward took its toll. Jill and Jojo complained of becoming groggy and tired, as the rhythmic strokes of His powerful wings began to rock them to sleep. Without any comment at all, Hooch quickly dropped off fast asleep, and began snoring like a combine.

"I can barely keep my eyes open," Jill said with a yawn, as she nestled herself amongst the silky warm neck feathers of Prince Tirips. "I think I'll just close my eyes for a minute or two." And with that, she was out cold.

"Yeah," mumbled Jojo, whose eyelids were becoming lead-heavy. "Me, too…I can barely keep my…" His words trailed off, as sleep hit him like a freight train.

Prince Tirips turned his head slightly to check on the Saints. He looked up and made eye contact with the Master Cherub. An all-knowing wink from Prince Tirips put a smile on Master Cherub's face. The Prince then turned back to the job at hand; the Celestial City of Mansoul would soon be in sight. It arrived quicker than expected. The powerful Woe-Bird, ridden by the mighty Kebatha, let out a piercing, ear shattering scream.

"What the…?!" shouted a startled Hooch, as he jerked upright from a sound sleep. "What was that?!"

"Are we going in to battle?" Jojo yelled, not sure why the Keba was making so much noise.

"Yeah!" exclaimed Jill, looking in every direction for any sign of trouble. Turning to Master Cherub she asked, "Is something wrong?"

Master Cherub just smiled. "No need to worry. That was not the battle cry of the Woe-Bird, but the Woe-Bird's call of delight, instead."

"Delight?! Delight?!" repeated Hooch. "You could have fooled me."

"What's he so excited about, anyway?" asked Jill, looking back to Master Cherub for an answer.

The answer he gave her came quickly and was brief. With a smile he said, "Behold!"

With that, all three Saints turned to see what had made the Woe-Bird so delirious with delight. It was the Celestial City, and they were headed straight for it!

The Celestial City of Mansoul

Even from a distance, the sheer grandeur and beauty of the Celestial City was evident. It appeared to float, as if on a bed of thick clouds, suspended amongst the stars. Light within the high walls, as far skyward as the Saints could see, emitted a vibrant green glow. The shimmering opaqueness of the walls, like that of the priceless gem Jasper, made visibility into the grand city impossible, though adding to its' colorful mystic. A pristine rainbow emanating over a thousand miles up illuminated the surrounding heavens as far as the eye could see. It was a majestic sight to behold.

"It's glorious!" exclaimed Jill, doing her best to hold back tears of joy, at the sight of a vision so breathtaking.

"It's huge!" exclaimed Jojo. "That's what it is. It goes on forever!"

"I'll say!" added Hooch, who asked, as the Prince guided them closer in for a better look. "Is that the entrance?"

"Yes, that's one of the three gates of the West Wall,"

explained Kebatha. "Prince Tirips is taking us to the main entrance of the Celestial City, located at the Northern Gates, many thousands of miles from here. While traversing our way around the city, we will fly as close to the walls as possible, for a better look."

As they approached the first of the three Western Gates, a huge being, similar to Kebatha in appearance, yet much larger, appeared to be guarding the entrance.

"And who, or *what,* is that?" asked Hooch.

"That," Master Cherub said, referring to an enormous ten-foot being with a spear, sword, and shield in hand, standing in front of the center gate, " is the Guardian of this gate."

"Wow!" exclaimed Jill. "I bet no one, I mean *no one*, gets by him without a pass."

"That would be a true statement, young daughter of the earth," said Kebatha, who was flying slightly to the left and rear of the Dove, out of reverence for the Prince. "Guardians of the Celestial City Gates have no fear."

"And the gate is so beautiful," commented Jill. "What is it made of?"

"Yeah," said Jojo. "And what is that writing on the gate? I don't think I've ever seen writing like that before."

"It ain't English!" blurted out Hooch. "I can tell you that much."

Question after question came in rapid fire. Master Cherub went on to explain that each of the gates was an enormous single pearl of perfection, with the name of one of the twelve nations of the Eno, whose people live within the city walls, written on it, in the language of the Eno.

"A language that you can't read…yet," said Master Cherub, with a smile.

"Ahhhhh," was all the Saints could muster. Jill though, just couldn't contain her exuberance at the size and beauty of the pearl.

"One pearl!" she exclaimed. "Talk about priceless! And the light from within makes it glow so beautifully!"

Hooch just rolled his eyes and mumbled something about, girls and jewelry, and asked about the structure of the city. "Why can't we see through the walls?" he asked, as all three Saints were anxious about getting a glimpse inside.

"The beautiful opaque green hue of the walls is due to the color of Jasper, the gem that makes up the walls," answered Master Cherub. "The Eno designed everything about the city to be of limitless beauty and strength, as well as completely private."

"And they look so thick," commented Jojo.

"The walls," continued Master Cherub, "are 200 feet thick. And…"

But before he could continue, Hooch interrupted. "You've got to be kidding? Those walls are two hundred feet thick? No way! That's over half a football field!"

"Yes," continued the ever patient Master Cherub, as Jojo and Jill just rolled their eyes in disbelief at the quickness with which Hooch did the math. "Two hundred feet, and each of the twelve layers of Jasper that make up that two hundred feet, has the name of one of Lord Nos' Faithful Twelve etched eternally on it."

"There's that number twelve again," commented Jojo curiously.

"Yeah, what do you mean by Faithful?" asked Jill.

"So many questions," laughed Master Cherub, as a surge from the mighty wings of Prince Tirips thrust them away from the West Wall and to those gates at the south. "It will be made known to you soon enough."

The three gates of the southern entrance flew rapidly by as the gates of the east came into view. Questions from the Saints swarmed Master Cherub like fireflies, as he kept answering with his usual tender patience and care. They passed the three gates of the east, and were closing in on the main entrance at the north. Upon leaving the Eastern Gates, Jojo asked about the city's immense size and height.

"Jojo, do you remember your sixth grade math teacher, Mrs. Frizit, and her lessons on geometric shapes?" asked Master Cherub with a smile.

"Well, Yes…and…Hey! How did you know she was my teacher?" he asked.

"Remember," went on Master Cherub, "We have had our eyes on you Saints for a very long time."

"I had her, too!" exclaimed Hooch, and then mumbled, "and I didn't like her much, either."

"Yes, Hooch," responded Master Cherub, "but she liked you enough to keep you in at recess to finish all of your work, didn't she?"

"Yeah, right, thanks for reminding me."

"And you still don't understand it!" shouted Jojo, as everyone had a good laugh.

As they neared the first of the Northern Gates, Jill was curious about Master Cherub's math question. "But what's Mrs. Frizit and her geometry lesson got to do with anything?"

"Good question," answered Master Cherub. "If you remember, one of those geometric shapes she discussed was called a cube."

"Right," said Jojo, "a shape with the same length, width, and height."

"Exactly," said Master Cherub. "And that is what the Celestial City of Mansoul is—a perfect cube." He went to explain that the shape of the city was exactly 1,500 miles in length, width, and height.

"Wow! 1,500 miles!" exclaimed Hooch. "That's about the length of the entire West Coast!"

"Upward and beyond, as well!" added Master Cherub, with a smile.

The Saints just shook their heads in amazement, finding it difficult to fathom such an enormous city, as they found themselves at the first of the three Northern Gates. Passing the first gate, Master Cherub answered what question he knew the Saints were thinking, "The main gate of all of the twelve gates of the Celestial City, is the middle of the three Northern Gates. The River of the Water of Life runs right to it. We will be coming upon it shortly."

The River of Life

As the Dove, Woe-Bird, and companions on board passed by the first of the three Northern Gates, the 400 miles separating it and the center gate went surprisingly fast.

"How is it that we can travel so far so fast?" asked Jill, as light from the city could be seen shining more clearly through the middle pearl gate the closer they got.

"Yeah," added Jojo, "it seems like we've traveled thousands of miles around this entire massive city in no time at all."

"You must remember," began Master Cherub, "you are no longer on earth. Time in the heavens is much different than you are used to on earth."

"What does *that* mean?" asked Hooch, as Master Cherub chuckled softly to himself.

"Time in the heavens, as well as on earth, is controlled by the Eno," said Master Cherub. "A minute in the heavens could be as that of an hour, week or year on earth. Just as if a minute were to pass on earth, it may seem as if years had passed in the High Heavens of the Eno. Is that making it any clearer?"

"*No*!" they all responded together.

"Ha!" Master Cherub laughed. "In time it will become crystal clear, just like the river we will be coming upon once we pass through the middle pearl gate."

The Saints had many more questions, but the sight of the middle pearl gate was right before them, and had their utmost attention. The Guardian of the gate had raised his spear and ordered them to halt. Prince Tirips flew in the lead with Kebatha close at his side, yet a respectful distance behind.

"*Who goes there*? *Who dares to come upon the northern entrance of the majestic and awesome Celestial City of Mansoul, and home of the Eno*? *Identify yourself*!"

As the Dove flew fearlessly into clear view, the Guardian dropped immediately to his gigantic knees and begged forgiveness.

"*My Prince, my Prince*! *Forgive me*!" bellowed the Guardian, with eyes never looking up, his head humbly bowed to his feet.

"Not to fear," said Prince Tirips. "Please, rise up, Judah, Great Guardian of the Northern Gate. It is good to see you, again!"

Kebatha maneuvered Keba closer to the Dove and whispered to the Saints, "Like I mentioned before, they fear no one, except those of the Eno."

"*Yes, and thank you, my Prince*!" answered the Guardian with his booming voice. "*And is that the great warrior, Kebatha, Captain of the Woe-Birds, and my dear friend, Master Cherub, overseer of all of Mid-Heaven, I see accompanying you*?"

"Yes it is," answered Prince Tirips.

Master Cherub gave a smile and bow of endearment, and Captain Kebatha and the Guardian placed their right fists across their hearts in a military salute of mutual respect.

"*So good to see you both*!" he bellowed with a smile.

"As it is to see you, my powerful friend!" replied Kebatha.

"Its good to be back to the glorious Celestial City of the Eno!" hailed Master Cherub with a wave and a smile.

These greetings would have continued for quite some time, if Prince Tirips had not interrupted. "And we have special guests, as well, for whom the Eno eagerly awaits," said Prince Tirips.

"*Very well, my Prince, enter at once and behold the River of Life that leads to the throne of Emperor Mai the Omni and His Son, Lord Nos*!"

With that said, and with a wave of his powerful arm, the enormous pearl gate swung open of its own accord. The brilliance of the light that shined forth from within the city walls stunned the Saints. They squinted and shielded their eyes with their hands from its brilliance.

"Whoa!" exclaimed Jojo, who received the brunt of the light's glory from where he sat towards the front. "It's like looking directly into the sun!"

"Your eyes will adjust!" shouted Captain Kebatha, as he saluted Prince Tirips and Master Cherub in preparation to leave. "It has been a pleasure to escort you both, and our young sons and daughter of the earth, to The Celestial City of Mansoul. It is time for me to return to my troops at Mid-Heaven."

"Farewell!" said the Dove and Master Cherub. "And thank you!"

The Saints waved goodbye, as Captain Kebatha wheeled Keba around, and headed back to Mid-Heaven. Keba let a Woe-Bird cry of delight, and like the wind, they were gone.

"I hate when he does that!" shouted Hooch, referring to the shrill cry of Keba that made him wince in pain. "But Captain Kebatha was right. My eyes have cleared up…my *ears* are killing me…but, yes, my eyes have cleared up."

Both Jojo and Jill laughed, as Prince Tirips dipped the flight of His path downward. The majesty and beauty of the River of Life came into better view. "It's beautiful!" they all shouted in unison, as Prince Tirips swooped down for an even closer view.

The River of Life was crystal clear—more pure and pristine in appearance than any mountain river or stream the Saints had ever seen. On each side of this great river were two gigantic fruit trees, covered with every sort of fruit imaginable.

"Look at those trees!" exclaimed Jill. "I've never seen so many different fruits on one tree!"

"I'm getting hungry just looking at them!" shouted Hooch, as Prince Tirips completed His descent to the level of the trees.

"These two trees," began Master Cherub, "are called the Trees of Life. They yield twelve different fruits each month."

"Oh, baby…baby…" moaned Hooch. "I'm starving! Could I go for one of those apples. Look at the size of those things!"

Prince Tirips, as if already knowing the hearts and thoughts of the Saints, had drifted within feet of the great tree. Master Cherub, as if on cue, deftly reached out and plucked a bright, luscious red apple and handed it to Hooch.

"All right!" shouted Hooch, as he chomped down on it with delight. "Thanks!" he yelled back at Master Cherub, as Jill and Jojo, asked, "May we?"

"Of course," said Master Cherub, as they both reached out in excitement.

"Got it!" shouted Jojo, grabbing an orange, the size of a volleyball, with both hands. He began to furiously peel away the skin. "I didn't know I was this hungry!"

But Jill was not quite so fortunate.

"Missed!" she yelled out, having reached for a delectable looking banana, and come up with an enormous leaf, instead. "Oh, my," she said dejectedly, making as though she were going to drop the leaf in dismay.

"Oh, no!" cautioned Master Cherub. "Hold on tight to that leaf."

Jill immediately put a tight grasp on the leaf that was easily as big as both her hands combined, while Master Cherub grabbed another banana the exact size of the one she had been reaching for. He passed it up to her, and she turned and thanked him with a smile.

"What's the big deal if she dropped the leaf?" asked Hooch, who was sitting closest to Master Cherub. "I mean, it *is* just a leaf, right?"

Both Jill and Jojo turned back to hear the answer, as Prince Tirips began His final turn round the immense tree, to start their journey up the River of Life to the Throne of the Eno.

"Yeah," said Jill, in between bites of the delicious banana that made her yearn for more. "I've got it right here in my hand, and it looks like any other leaf I've ever seen, only bigger."

"The Tree of Life only permits individuals to take from it what it pleases them to have," answered Master Cherub. "And it was meant for Jill, and Jill alone, to have that leaf."

"Okay, okay," began Jojo, a bit frustrated at the answer. "I don't even want to know *how* the tree would know what was taken, or not taken. I'm just curious as to what makes the leaf so special? What made you so concerned that she might drop it?'

"The leaves of the Trees of Life have special healing powers," began Master Cherub. "The Tree permitted Jill to take from it, something that only a special few are able to do. It is a very great gift. There is a very great honor coming her way."

After Master Cherub's brief explanation a barrage of questions from the Saints ensued. Questions about what all of the fruits were, how come one piece of fruit seemed to fill them up so completely, how did they get so big, did someone have to eat the leaf to be healed, what kind of healing did it do, and so on.

"All will be made known to you in due time," he answered, "in due time."

"That's what you *always* say!" exclaimed Hooch impatiently. Prince Tirips completed his final turn around the Tree of Life, now on a direct path towards the Throne of the Eno. The turn was a tight one, causing the Saints, especially Hooch, to grab a hold of the Prince tightly.

"Whoa!" exclaimed Hooch, as the Dove shot a piercing glance his way, a glance that implied the Prince was not happy at Hooch's tone of disrespect and impatience toward Master Cherub.

"Okay...okay," replied Hooch, sheepishly. "I get it, I get it, in due time...in due time."

The Dove replied with a thank you and a smile, and pressed forward upriver. The River of Life flowed at a speedy rate, but never created a ripple; it ran smooth as glass and never seemed to empty anywhere or overflow the riverbank. No part or drop of the river ever left the city, yet it flowed right up to the city gates. These interesting tidbits didn't escape the ever curious eyes of the Saints. In between bites of the tastiest fruits they'd ever eaten, the incessant questions began again.

"How come," began Jill, "the river never seems to end? When we flew through the gate, I didn't see any water running out of the city? Where does it go?"

"Yeah," piped in Jojo, "it flows and flows yet it never ends."

"Weird!" exclaimed Hooch. "But cool!"

Master Cherub began to answer, but Jojo interrupted; he was pointing at the riverbank. What are all of those huge buildings? There must be thousands of them!"

Both Hooch and Jill turned in the direction he was pointing and were equally amazed. "They're on this side, as well!" shouted Hooch. "They look like castles!"

Jill kept her comments to herself, content to quietly take in all of the wonders around her. She was especially mesmerized by how many castles there were—more than she could number—stacked up to the top of the city, as high as she could see. "It's as if they were hung on air," she quietly commented to herself.

Though Hooch and Jojo, in constant chatter between themselves, didn't hear her comment, Master Cherub, as was his want, did. He chose at this time, though, to remain silent, and let the magnificence of the city speak for itself. Besides, the Throne of the Eno, their final destination, was now in sight.

The Throne of the Eno

"Look!" exclaimed Jill. "What *is* that?"

All three Saints went silent and stared up ahead of them. Master Cherub clarified what it was they were approaching.

"That," began Master Cherub, "is the Throne of the Eno!"

The magnificence, even from a distance, took their breath away. Oohs and aahs were all that could be expressed. And even those moans of delight went silent as Prince Tirips headed right toward what looked like a waterfall directly in front of them.

"Whoa!" shouted Hooch, as a collision with the waterfall looked assuredly imminent. "This could be interesting!"

"All is well," assured Master Cherub, in a tone that always had a peaceful and comforting effect on the Saints. "Now, hold on tight."

The Saints obediently grabbed tighter to the feathers of the Prince, as the steep ascent up the waterfall began. Up flew the Dove, effortlessly climbing to their destination.

The waterfall had more of a glacial sense about it, as not a drop or spray was out of place. Smoothly and continuously it flowed beneath them. Jill's eyes began to tear up with sadness that such beauty as the river had to end. But that emotion quickly turned to awesome wonder at the sight before her. At the top, all three Saints went speechless.

Prince Tirips turned and said, "We've arrived!"

He gently landed at the foot of the throne. Master Cherub and the children slid off His back with ease. They gathered themselves at the bottom step, unsure of what was to take place next. Then, as if from nowhere, yet blaring from everywhere, a voice of cascading waterfalls thundered forth.

"*I am King Mai the Omni. Welcome... Welcome sons and daughter of earth, to the Celestial City of Mansoul!*" He bellowed.

The Saints dropped to their knees in fear.

"And I, Lord Nos, Son of King Mai, greet you, oh worthy Saints of 31st Street!"

Lord Nos's voice was similar to that of Prince Tirips, yet different.

"Now, follow with your eyes," Lord Nos continued, "the flight of Prince Tirips to the Throne of the Eno!"

And with that, the once enormous Dove that had carried them these many thousands of miles was once again the size of the little Dove that they first had met. The Saints, though, still shaken with fear at the overwhelming magnificence surrounding them, kept their heads bowed with eyes looking down. It wasn't until Lord Nos spoke again, that they took courage to gaze upward.

"Fear not, look up, and behold the flight of Prince Tirips."

The Saints, emboldened by the comforting words of Lord Nos, watched as Prince Tirips flew up the twenty-four steps, and perched Himself on the left shoulder of Lord Nos, the mighty being standing to the right of the throne. On the throne itself, was seated King Mai, a being of such wonder and majesty that His brilliance emanated forth like that of a thousands suns. It struck awe and fear in the Saints, making it impossible for them to look in His glorious direction.

"*Listen to my Son*!" thundered King Mai. "*Into His hands do I bequeath all authority*! *Listen to him and obey*!"

And with that, King Mai vanished, and the throne was empty. Lord Nos, with Prince Tirips perched on His shoulder, remained.

"Please, come forward!" said the Lord, beckoning the Saints up the steps towards him.

Master Cherub urged them forward, but he himself remained behind.

"Aren't you coming?" questioned Jill in a concerned tone of voice.

"I will remain behind for now. I will come forward when I am summoned. Now, go, and have no fear," he encouraged with a smile. "Lord Nos, the beloved, beckons you."

The Saints turned back to the steps, and looked up at Lord Nos, a towering majestic figure. He was dressed in a robe that fell to His feet, with a golden sash around His chest. His head and hair were white like wool, as white as snow; and His eyes blazed like fire. Hooch's entire body began to go limp, causing him to catch his toe and stumble ever so slightly. "Oops," he said bashfully, as both Jojo and Jill helped him to his feet. "Sorry about that."

As they made their way closer to the top, Lord Nos spoke again, causing all three Saints to fall at His feet—feet like bronze glowing in a furnace. His face, like King Mai, was like the sun shining in all its brilliance. Yet, unlike King Mai, the Saints were permitted to look upon Lord Nos freely, and with no fear.

"Please rise, o sons of the earth!" He commanded. The powerful yet soothing tone in which He spoke empowered them with courage, while simultaneously striking reverential fear in their hearts. "I've been awaiting your arrival with great anticipation!"

The Saints rose slowly, and meekly began to introduce themselves. But Lord Nos held up His mighty hand, and stopped them. "No need for introductions," He began. "I've known you before your birth, and it is I who directed you here by way of Prince Tirips, fellow partner of the Eno. Please, sons of the earth, sit at the foot of the great Throne of the Eno."

And with that, Lord Nos took his place upon the throne that His father, King Mai the Omni, had vacated. The question in the minds of the Saints as to where He had disappeared was quickly answered. As they seated themselves, King Mai, though His physical presence unseen, thundered once again. "*This is my Son, in whom I am well pleased! Listen to Him and live*!"

And then there was silence.

"I don't know if I can take much more of this," sighed Hooch, shaking noticeably.

"This has to be a dream…It just has to be! Somebody pinch, hit me…something! I just gotta wake up!"

"It is no dream, young son of the earth," said Lord Nos, reaching forward and putting his powerful hand on Hooch's shoulder. "You will be fine."

The touch of Lord Nos settled the usually fearless and powerful Hooch in an instant. It was a calm and peace that overcame him; something he had never experienced before, and would never forget. And, as Lord Nos had promised, he was fine. An impatient Jojo, though, was not.

"If I may ask," Jojo said, in a tone indicating his impatience, "what exactly the reason is as to why we're here. I mean, I know we had reasons when we ran away from the orphanage last night, but to end up here, wherever here really is, standing before your Majesty as we are, is confusing to me. We're just a bunch of scared, know nothing orphans in search of answers. Will we ever know those answers? Will you please help us?"

"Yes, Lord Nos," Jill added. "You know everything. You know our purpose in escaping the orphanage was to discover the truth about Jojo's parents. And now, in addition to that, we must also rescue Gus from the clutches of the Underlings—those dupes of the dreaded Cardinal Eslaf Tehprop. As well as find out why all of the orphans at the 31st Street Orphanage, after age twelve, are turned into something other than themselves by the evil Cardinal.

"It feels like we're spinning our wheels," added Hooch. "And we just don't have time to do that. We're running out of time."

Lord Nos listened patiently then raised His hand for quiet. "You are quite right, my young children of the earth. Your journey so far has been a difficult and intense ordeal," said Lord Nos. "It is right and proper that everything be made known to you at this time."

All of the Saints let out a sigh of relief and said, "Thank you!"

"It is now time," continued Lord Nos, "for me to reveal the real reason you were called."

The Reveal

The Saints leaned forward in anticipation as to what Lord Nos would reveal to them about why they were called. Prince Tirips flew from the shoulder of the Lord, and alighted on the back of the Great Throne.

"Long ago," began Lord Nos, "in a time before time, my Father, Emperor Mai the Omni, had great designs for a creation of a race that would, of their own free will, follow the Eno and Our ways. This following was to occur with little or no interference on Our part at all. This task, of creating this race and the world they were to inhabit, my Father put into my hands, and I joyfully and faithfully accepted it."

Lord Nos went on to explain how the Eno already had tens, hundreds, and thousands of thousands of servants who obeyed as created servants were *made* to obey. They had no free will to choose otherwise. Their will to obey the Eno without reservation was imputed into their being. One very powerful servant desired to change this. His name was Natas.

"The most beautiful, perfect, and first created of these servants was High Servant Natas. There were no servants like him; he was the favorite of the Eno in all respects," said Lord Nos. "He, along with the second in command, Vice-Commander Leahcim, second created and most powerful servant of the Eno, ruled the other servants in the High Heavens. And there was perfect harmony."

He went to explain how with the High Heavens now in perfect order, it was time to tend to His task at hand: to create an order of free will beings to be placed on the earth. These were to be humans who would be given the opportunity to choose the ways of the Eno of their own free will, or not. A test, if you will, of those truly desiring the Eno.

"In my creation, I made sure that the climate, vegetation, food, and water on earth were abundant and perfect," said Lord Nos. "All the created beings were given a brilliance of mind to create their own world, without any interference from the Eno, and to make a choice to follow and obey the Eno, *completely* of their own free will."

"But how were they to choose the ways of the Eno, if they had no knowledge of you? That seems a bit unfair, don't you think?" Jill asked.

"Excellent question, daughter of earth," said Lord Nos, who then went on to answer her question to the fullest.

"Into the created human being, as I said, I placed a powerful intelligence. Along with that intelligence, I imparted unto them a spirit and soul, that yearned for the Eno," He continued. "With this desire for the Eno in place humans would then be able, if they so chose, to also draw from earthly surroundings the fact that something greater than themselves was at work. It would then be their decision as to whether or not they would, totally of their free will, accept, or reject, the Eno."

"Oh, I get it," interrupted Jojo. "I see what you mean about the surroundings providing an answer. I've had thoughts like that before. Like, how we all came to be here in the first place? And how whether or not the earth and all of the galaxies just happened to form all by themselves, or was there some higher authority behind it all? And was it *just* by coincidence that the sun was made to rise exactly the same way everyday? And was it just by chance that the moon and stars continually pop out at precisely the appropriate time every night, to light up the darkness? And no matter how hard the rains fall, is it mere happenstance that the oceans never overflow? And..."

"And," blurted in Hooch, "was it luck that the earth was placed just close enough to the sun so as to not burn up, but not too far away to freeze? And..."

"And were humans given the ability, just out of the blue," piped in Jill, "to heal themselves, and to procreate?"

This went on for quite some time until Lord Nos interrupted them by exclaiming, "Exactly!"

He then proceeded to unveil to the Saints, how all of creation was so clearly defined as having been created by something far greater and more powerful than themselves, that it would take a concerted desire of the will, by all humans, *not* to believe it to be fact.

"Or, the fact that they're just not very bright!" laughed Jojo, as Lord Nos then unveiled why believing for many became so difficult.

He told of an incident that changed the course of His designs for earth forever. "It happened in a manner of great deceit and stealth," He said. "Unbeknownst to any of the High Heavens, Natas, and one third of the Heavenly Host, grew tired of obedience to the Eno. They became envious of what they called the 'puny human race' and their free will, and wanted for themselves that same free will to choose and control their own lives and destiny. Under the leadership of the traitor High Servant Natas, they began devising a plot to overthrow the Eno. But before the plot came to fruition, Natas, in a daring act that caused his demise, broke the cardinal rule of the Eno; he willfully had personal contact with a human, a woman, and impregnated her."

"He did *what*?" asked Jill. "Can that happen?"

"It can," stated Lord Nos, "and did."

"How is that possible?" asked Jojo. "I mean, we're flesh and blood, and the created servants are, well, *not* flesh and blood. It's pretty clear, we're not the same. I mean, what kind of child did they have?"

"And who was the woman?" asked Jill.

"The woman, whose name will remain unknown forever has been forgiven and resides in the land of Mid-Heaven. It is there that all of the true faithful of the Eno who survived the Great Deception and Fall remain to this very day. They remain there until it is their time to journey to the Celestial City of Mansoul."

"Falling in love, as she did, with someone as bad as Natas is anything but being faithful to the Eno," commented Hooch. "Why was she forgiven?"

"Point well taken," said Lord Nos. "Natas, once a shining

light, became the worst of the worst of all creation. He has been around longer than all of the created Host. Only the Eno has existed for a longer time. He used the knowledge and understanding imparted to him by the Eno to lure and mesmerize the woman into that unthinkable act. Therefore, because she was no match for his wiles and cunning, she was forgiven. But High Servant Natas was not, and never will be."

"What happened to him?" asked Jill. "Something incredibly unpleasant, I hope?"

"Yeah," blurted in Hooch, "please tell us it was something *really* bad."

Lord Nos explained how Natas and his evil followers were banished to the bowels of inner earth, a prison across the River Sedah, for a thousand years. He was locked up with only Lord Nos having the key to his prison. Natas' evil horde was given permission to tend to him and do his bidding which consisted of gathering grubs, insects, worms, and any other vile form of sustenance needed for his survival."

"Now *that's* what I'm talking about!" exclaimed Hooch. "Make it hurt! Gotta make it hurt!"

Master Cherub smiled and then continued. "And all of the evil horde while tending to Natas, were never to leave the bowels of inner earth. If for some reason they did make their way to upper earth, special precautions by the Eno were taken."

"And what precaution was that?" asked Jill.

"The evil horde," went on Lord Nos, "including Natas, were branded in such a way, that if by chance they did succeed to escape the Nether World below, they would instantly be discovered."

"What type of brand was that?" asked Jojo.

"They were all cursed with the head of a snake—the most vile, insidious creature on earth."

"A *what* kind of head?" asked Jojo. "Did I hear you say a snake's head?"

"That is correct," said Lord Nos, as He calmly added, "like you saw in the Cardinal's office."

"I knew it!" shouted Jojo. "I was sure that it was a snake's head on the Cardinal, and that other Priest, too. For a while there I thought I was going crazy!"

"We did, too!" yelled Hooch. "This is good news."

"Hey," said Jill, "we never told you about Jojo seeing the Cardinal's snake head. How did you know about that?"

"Remember, the Eno knows all," Lord Nos stated matter-of-factly.

"Oh, yeah," said Jill sheepishly. "You'd think I would have figured that out by now. I'm so sorry. Forgive me."

Lord Nos just smiled and said, "Daughter of earth, you were forgiven before you asked."

Jill, as well as Hooch and Jojo, paused in thought as a brief moment of quiet ensued. The weight of what Lord Nos said, of the Eno knowing all, filled each one of them with an overwhelming peace. A peace, though, quickly broken by Jojo's inquiring mind.

"What *does* it all, mean?" asked Jojo. "How many of those snake-headed creatures are there? And where does that leave us? Is the quest to all of our answers centered around the snake-heads, that evil horde of Natas?"

"Yeah," said Hooch. "This is getting pretty weird. I mean, now we've got to battle snake people, or what?"

"And, how did the Cardinal become a snake person, anyway? And how is he connected with Natas?" asked Jill. "Did the baby the woman gave birth to have anything to do with all of this?"

"Yeah," asked Jojo. "What about him? What happened to the little guy?"

Lord Nos paused and became very quiet. After a moment or two, just as the Saints were about to ask Him the question again, Prince Tirips flew from His perch atop the Great Throne behind Lord Nos. He headed down the stairs in front of the Great Throne, to speak to Master Cherub, who was waiting at the bottom step.

"I am having Prince Tirips invite my faithful servant Master Cherub at this time," said Lord Nos to the Saints. "He will speak about the twins that were born to that woman."

"*Twins*?" exclaimed the Saints in unison, as Master Cherub made his way up the steps and over to the side of the Great Throne beside Lord Nos. Prince Tirips took his place, once again, behind Lord Nos.

"Welcome, Master Cherub, my good friend and faithful servant," said Lord Nos. "Please stand next to me and speak to the Saints of the woman and her twins."

"Yes, my Lord," answered Master Cherub. "It would be my honor."

Master Cherub humbly moved next to Lord Nos, and began telling the story of how a wonderful loving woman was tricked, deceived with lies into falling in love with the wicked Natas. "The unnamed woman that Lord Nos referred to is my mother," began Master Cherub.

The Saints sat speechless. No one moved. No one spoke.

All eyes were riveted on Master Cherub, hanging on his every word. Master Cherub glanced over at Lord Nos who nodded His approval to continue.

"When my mother gave birth, my father, Natas, was there. He knew the exact minute the birth was to occur. He planned that at the moment of my brother's birth he would be there, so that he could snatch him from my mother. My mother was helpless to save my brother."

"How come he didn't get you, too?"

"At the precise moment of my brother's birth, my father, as planned, arrived with the evil horde and stole him from my mother's arms. He and his evil followers made haste to hide from the Eno in the deep caverns that exist in the Reinar Mountains. Unknown to him, was that as soon as they departed, leaving my mother to fend for herself and eventually die, she gave birth to a second child—me. It was at that time, tired and weak from giving birth, that she was able to flee and hide me in the area encompassed by a great mist. The place that eventually became the entrance to Mid-Heaven."

"You mean the same land of the mist and Great Oak Tree that led us to you?" asked Jill.

"Precisely," answered Master Cherub. "It was at that spot that the animals of the mist, those extraordinary creatures of kindness and compassion, aided and protected my mother and me."

"You mean Whitsnit, Quidley, and the others?" asked Jojo.

"No, they were not born, yet. It was their ancestors. Whitsnit's great-grandfather, Whithertwit, was the leader of them all that found and cared for us. If not for the creatures of the mist, we never would have survived."

"Could they talk like they do now?" asked Hooch.

"No," smiled Master Cherub. "It was not until I had grown to adulthood, in human years, that I taught them to speak. Until that time, they nurtured my mother and me through their acts of kindness and caring, but with no speaking."

"Did you go immediately up to Mid-Heaven?" asked Jill.

"It was not until I was an adolescent, about your age, that the way up through the Great Oak was revealed to me," he went on. "It was as if the animals knew the appropriate time to guide us to the shaft, where the ancestors of Captain Bushtail and his other multitudinous squirrel cousins flew us on that furry carpet ride to the land above."

"Oh, man!" shouted Hooch. "Wow! Was that ride awesome, or what?"

All of the Saints briefly reminisced about the ride to Mid-Heaven, as Jill then asked a question they were all wondering about.

"What happened to your brother? Was he in the mountains the entire time?"

"Yes," asked Jojo. "And I thought you said that Natas was immediately thrown into prison in Syba. How did your brother survive, if he was just a little baby, without the help of his father?"

Master Cherub explained that when the Eno heard of Natas' treasonous act against them, they immediately dispatched the New Commander of the Heavenly Host's armies, Commander Leahcim, to the Mountains of Reinar to capture my father and his evil horde.

"It was in the Mountains of Reinar, behind and to the north of Chewela, where Natas and his followers, before being captured, had time to curse all of the mountains and the animals of the area under an evil spell," said Master Cherub. "The wolves, mountain lions, snakes, and accursed ten-foot tall Toofgibs, those man-beasts that to this day roam the mountains feeding on all flesh, human or otherwise, were put under his spell. It was they who hid the baby in the mountain caves, and cared for him until he was of age to leave, out of sight of Commander Leahcim and his soldiers of the Heavenly Host."

"What do you mean when you said Natas cursed all of the mountains?" asked Jojo. "I mean, I understand somewhat cursing the animals, but how did he curse the mountains?"

"Good question, Jojo," continued Master Cherub. "And it's good information to know if you ever happen to wander that way by mistake, as the curse on those mountains still remains to this day. Natas put a specially crafted curse that has the rivers, trees, and even the rocks obeying his every command. It is a place to avoid at all cost as evil, and evil alone, is the rule of the day in that area."

"What sort of things do they do?" asked Hooch. "I've never been in mountains that were cursed…haunted…or whatever."

"And it is my hope that you never do," continued Master Cherub. "For you may find yourself napping under the shade of a giant cursed fir tree, only to discover you've become intertwined in its thick branches that silently squeeze the life from you. Or rivers that appear shallow enough to cross, but turn to quick sand and swallow you in a slow, suffocating death. Not to speak of the deep rivers that can turn an innocent afternoon swim in smooth, quiet waters into a raging nightmare of swirling tide pool waters spinning and sucking you to the bottom of who knows where. And the rocks…"

Hooch quickly interrupted, "Okay! Okay! Enough already! We get the picture!"

"It's amazing to me that with all of that evil around, that your twin had a chance of surviving at all," said Jill. "He was not only raised by evil animals, but was surrounded by evil on all sides. How, awfully, sad!"

"Yes," said Master Cherub. "He was born evil and raised by evil. And…he is lost forever in his evil ways to this very day."

"Do you know where he is, today?" inquired Hooch.

"Yeah," asked Jojo, "is he anywhere we might know?"

Master Cherub paused thoughtfully then replied, "Not only do you know *where* he is, but you know *who* he is. My twin brother is the wicked Cardinal Essey!"

"No way!" exclaimed Hooch. "Talk about the black sheep of the family!"

"I see what you mean by him being lost forever," said Jill.

"Though, Jill," interjected Lord Nos, "the opportunity to turn from his evil ways still does exist. He, as with all humans, though he is only half human, would be given all of the rights to resist evil and accept the ways of the Eno, if he ever chose to do so."

"Wouldn't it be difficult, my Lord, for the Cardinal to return to the Eno?" asked Jill. "I mean, his father's evil hold on him is so powerful. Would it really be possible for him to leave?"

"All things are possible with the Eno," stated Lord Nos, as he glanced at Master Cherub with a smile. "All things are possible."

"I'm just curious, after coming of age and leaving the protection and care of the animals of the mountains of Reniar, how was it possible for the Cardinal to continue following Natas, while he was locked away in the Great Pit of Syba?" asked Jojo.

"Yeah," piped in Hooch. "How could Natas communicate with the Cardinal from the bowels of earth? That just doesn't seem possible."

"Quite right," continued Master Cherub, as he went on to remind the Saints that though Natas was bolted and chained in the Great Pit, unable to move freely, his other traitorous comrades, now a very active Sybian Horde, were not. They were permitted by the Eno to serve Natas, though still under the earth, and do his bidding. The only restraint was that they could *never* be permitted outside of Syba. Therefore, the entrance in and out of Syba was guarded by two powerful Guardians of the Eno who were to have made it *impossible* to cross over the River Sedah to upper earth."

"Well," interrupted Hooch, "has anything happened to change that?"

"Yes, something terrible happened that made the once impossible act of crossing over to upper earth a reality," continued Master Cherub. "Somehow, those of the Sybian Horde are now able to sneak up from the underworld and cross the River Sedah totally unnoticed."

"Even with the Eno's Guardians protecting the entire area? How is that possible?" asked Jill.

"The reason for the Sybian's ability to escape is known only to the Eno," answered Lord Nos. "We have withheld that knowledge from the servants of the Eno, including the

Guardians, and have chosen you, the 31st Street Saints to be used to glorify Us in leading the vanguard against Natas and his horde. We will clarify this to a greater degree at the appropriate time."

The Saints went silent, humbled at such an honor.

"Just realize that now," continued Lord Nos, "it is *imperative* that the answer to this mystery, as well as the answer to where the *exact* entry point being used to enter upper earth is located, be answered by you…and it must be done quickly."

"I thank you for bestowing this great honor on us," said Jill. "I'm am bewildered somewhat that you, the all powerful Eno, would need to choose us, but I thank you all the same. I am curious, though, as to where this entry point may be?"

Lord Nos smiled at her and nodded toward Master Cherub to continue.

"At the mouth of the River Sedah," stated Master Cherub without hesitation.

"And, if I may ask, where *is* this River?" asked Jojo.

"You may," answered Master Cherub. "The River Sedah is located where few people on earth would ever think to look—somewhere out of the way, and totally remote."

"Someplace so remote and out of the way like Chewela, maybe?" said Jojo in facetious tone. "I mean, who would ever think to look there for something important, right?"

Hooch wasn't buying that explanation. "Naaawwww," he said. "I've never seen or heard of any river like that, no way."

"The fact is you are quite right, Jojo." Master Cherub continued. "That is very perceptive of you."

Jojo thanked Master Cherub, who then went on to explain that the mouth of the River Sedah was at the base behind the cascading waterfall of Chewela; a waterfall formed by the mighty rushing rivers flowing from the cursed Mountains of Reinar.

"Hey!" exclaimed Jill. "That's right behind the Cathedral, isn't it?"

"Precisely," said Master Cherub. "And the entrance behind the waterfall has remained there, unnoticed and untouched, for these many years. And then something happened in the last fifty years or so. Do you know what that is?"

"Well," said Jojo, "the town remodeled the Cathedral, before we were born, when the Cardinal arrived. Or that's what my dad told me before…" His voice trailed off, and he became very silent at the thought of his missing mother and dad.

"Yes," said Master Cherub, looking at Jojo. "And the Cardinal, my evil twin, has been remodeling not only on the outside, but from within, as well. He has been very busy, very busy indeed."

"What do you mean 'from within, as well'?" asked Jill. "Is there some connection between the waterfall entrance to the River Sedah and inside the Cathedral?"

"We think that may be the case," said Master Cherub. "A massive excavation beneath the Cathedral, two stories down, was completed just before the cleansings became a major push by Cardinal Essey."

"What were they excavating for?" asked Hooch. " If it was that big of a deal there must have been some reason given as to what was going on. Somebody must have asked something, don't you think?"

"There were questions," answered Master Cherub.

"Many of them, as it was a very lengthy and expensive project. When money is involved, people tend to get suspicious. But the Cardinal was quick to answer any questions and quell all suspicions. He is a master at putting his parishioner's minds to rest."

"How did he do that?" asked Jojo.

"He had the Cathedral Information Priest immediately inform all Saint Barnabus Parishioners that a special holding area, a wine cellar if you will, was being built to contain all of the holy wine that had been blessed by the Bishop of Wonderous Miracles and turned into the blood of Jesus. It was built that far below ground, for protection from thieves and heretics, or that's what the people were told. And, it is located at the same end of the Cathedral as the waterfall."

"And as always," smirked Hooch, "no one but the Cardinal and his Sanctified Priests are ever permitted into that area, right?"

"Exactly," said Master Cherub with a smile. "And the cleansings started at the time of the wine cellar's completion."

"Interesting, isn't it, that the timing of these cleansings and the completion of the wine cellar coincide so closely," began Jojo. "If there is a connection between the entrance to the River Sedah and the wine cellar, and it appears that would be a logical assumption, then that is precisely where our search should begin."

"Yes, and if you're right Jojo," said Master Cherub, "the danger in the area will be immense. The volume of Sybians traveling back and forth could be staggering. Add to that the massive numbers of individuals who have become Underlings through the Cardinal's cleansings, and Natas may very well have himself a powerful army, indeed."

“I know what you mean,” continued Jojo. “Because of those cleansings of Cardinal Essey’s, it’s going to be hard to even know how many are under Natas’ control, let alone how the Cardinal is doing it. You’re brother, Master Cherub, has been very active. And the evil plan of Natas will soon be upon us.”

“That’s correct,” said Master Cherub, in a somber tone. “Time is of the essence.”

“Something needs to be done about all of this evil on earth, and it appears this task has been laid in our laps. I, for one, am willing to do anything to stop it,” said Hooch. “Especially, if it means the opportunity to free Gus from the evil clutches of that fiend, Cardinal Essey, and his cohorts in crime!”

“And not only Gus, but we must find out what happened to Jojo’s parents, as well as free all of the innocent kids from the orphanage that have been turned into Underlings. The curse they are under must be broken,” added Jill.

“I agree,” said Jojo. “And we’ll find a way. We have to!”

Lord Nos, smiling at the enthusiasm of the 31st Street Saints, rose slowly from His throne, in preparation to speak. Master Cherub sat next to the Saints at the foot of the throne.

“It is time,” began Lord Nos, “for the mystery behind your call to this place be revealed.”

The Mystery

As Master Cherub and the Saints sat obediently before the Throne of the Eno, events of wonder ensued. Prince Tirips ceased from appearing as a Dove and took the form of an angelic being: similar to that of Lord Nos, yet not. The Prince took his place to the left of the throne. Lord Nos took His right and glorious position to the right hand of the throne, closest to his Father's heart.

The Saints trembled at what was unfolding before them. The three separate beings of the Eno slowly began to merge together, becoming one voluminous cloud at the center of the throne. Bolts of lightening and ear shattering bursts of thunder exploded throughout.

"Bow your heads," declared Master Cherub, "and behold the Eno!"

The Saints needed no encouragement to bow in reverence, and they did not look up until they were bidden to do so. Holding each other's hands, they waited in fear, not knowing what to expect next. What happened next quickly replaced their fear and concern with peace and joy.

"Be not afraid," commanded the Eno. "Look upon Us, as we unfold the mystery of why you were summoned here."

The Saints and Master Cherub did as they were told, slowly lifting their eyes upward.

Squinting at first, they prepared for the brilliance they had previously experienced. To their astonishment, they were able to look upon the Eno with eyes wide open. The thunder and lightening had given way to a gentle flickering fog.

"We know, that while imprisoned in Syba, the land located in the deepest bowels of inner earth, for the past 999 years, Natas and his followers have kept very busy," began the Eno. "Evil, as you know, never rests, and is ever diligent. Natas' Sybian Horde discovered, while scrounging around for grubs, worms, and other vile filth to feed their master, a special mineral. This very special mineral, when heated to an intense heat, and combined with other minerals found only in the bowels of inner earth, could be used to create a potion of invisibility when consumed. It was in this way that the Sybians were able to slip past the Guardians of the Eno, back across the River Sedah, to upper earth."

"Oh, great," moaned Hooch.

"Shhhhhh," said Jill, gently touching Hooch's arm.

"For you see, We informed Commander Leahcim, Commander of the Heavenly Host, that while under the influence of the potion, these Sybian's were in spirit form only," the Eno continued. "We commanded Leahcim and his armies to observe, but not intervene. We soon discovered that these Sybians could move freely about as the wind, but had no physical capabilities at all. Though they might whisper evil thoughts in the minds of unknowing humans, and even speak to them audibly to confuse or disrupt their minds, they were not able to *physically* have any effect on them at all."

Slowly, and respectfully, Jojo raised his hand requesting to speak.

"Yes, son of earth?" asked the Eno. "Please speak."

"You mean they could come right up next to anyone and put a thought in their head, without them even knowing?" Jojo asked. "Yet, they were unable to touch or physically harm anyone, either?"

"That is correct, son of earth," replied the Eno, as Jill timidly rose her hand to speak.

"Please speak, daughter of earth."

"Very respectfully, if that's the case, then what is the concern?" Jill asked, working up the courage to delve deeper into this riddle. "It appears to me that the Sybian Horde, though vile and corrupt and deserving of annihilation, is basically harmless to anyone of a pure heart and mind. Why worry about them if they just drift around the earth, aimlessly and harmlessly, as ghosts?"

"This was the case for many years," the Eno went on. "But that is not quite the case anymore. The wicked son of Natas, Cardinal Eslaf, has made sure or that."

The Eno continued to explain that through the genius of Cardinal Essey, having the genetic make-up of a half-immortal servant of the Eno, he discovered a way to hide the evil snake head presence that has cursed all of the Sybian Horde. He found a way that now permits them to move freely around the earth in *physical* human form. And for the past fifty years, no one human had been the wiser.

"Oh, no, this can't be! No one on earth will be safe," cried Jill.

"That is correct, daughter of earth," answered the Eno. "And time is running out. The thousand-year prison term of Natas, and his Sybian Horde, is at hand. He must be stopped before he and the Sybian Horde are freed to join his growing followers of upper earth Underlings."

"But, once again, and I beg You not to take this the wrong way, but can't you stop them?" pleaded Jojo. "I mean…No one is more powerful than the Eno."

After Jojo's question, there was silence from the Eno that seemed to last forever. Then with great patience and care, their response was given, as They clarified in more detail, as They said They would.

"Before the fall of Natas and his evil followers," began the Eno, "it was decided that in order to be sure that the followers of the Eno were *true* followers, no interference on our part could ever take place."

"But what about us?" asked Hooch "You chose us to come, didn't you?"

"Ah, son of earth," continued the Eno, "there truly is no guile in you. But all of you, chosen as you were, accepted of your free will, every step of the way. No one forced you to come; though we knew you would. You came of your own accord."

"We did come of our free will, and as for me I know I made the right choice." stated Jojo.

Both Hooch and Jill wholeheartedly agreed. "I do have one question, though," asked Jill. "How did you know we would accept?"

"We know the hearts and minds of all humans; those who will accept and those who will not. We knew the goodness that existed in your hearts, and what your final decision would be."

"Now that we know there's a problem of earth shattering proportions about to occur upon Natas' release," stated Jojo, "my question to you, most respectfully, is how are we three orphans supposed to be of any help and bring glory to You, as You mentioned earlier, especially when it comes to battling immortal creatures like Natas, and his Sybian Horde?"

No answer to Jojo's question was given. Instead, the Eno slowly became a dark and foreboding cloud before them. The bursts of thunder and lightening returned. The Saints and Master Cherub bowed in fear and reverence.

"Oh, great, nice going, Jojo," whispered Hooch. "Now you've really gone and done it."

The Eno remained hovering before them, for what seemed an eternity. Afraid to look up, they remained with bowed heads, trembling, until the command to rise was given.

"*Rise before the great and powerful Eno, oh sons and daughter of earth*!"

The Saints, with quivering nerves and unsteady knees, rose to their feet; their eyes still looking downward waiting obediently for the next command.

"In answer to your question, son of earth, We pose a question to the three of you," began the Eno. "Do you agree to set aside your fears and trust in the Eno, no matter what the outcome? To accept on faith alone, and obediently comply with our demands without question, before even hearing what it is we require of you?"

The Saints glanced into each other's eyes still trembling. They squeezed each other's hands tighter. A peace came over each of them, almost simultaneously. It was as if at that very moment they could read each other's hearts and minds, and in an instant, the answer was obvious to all of them.

With a boldness they had heretofore never experienced, they rose to their feet, raised their eyes, and answered in unison, "*We do*!"

"Ahhhh!!" exclaimed the Eno. "We have chosen well! Now, the mission before you, Saints of 31st Street, is to seek out and discover the method Natas and his Sybian Horde are using to sneak the dreaded snakeheads across the River Sedah. Find the manner in which they are escaping from the bowels of the earth before the termination of their thousand-year banishment. Discover and expose the process they are using to create their Underling Army that Natas and his Sybian Horde plan to use against the Eno upon their release."

"Do you accept this task before you?"

And again, as before, they boldly answered, "*We do*!"

"To assist you on your mission, we have special gifts that will help you along the way," continued the Eno. "To you, Jojo, the unwritten leader of the Saints, we give the Ring of Foresight, Wisdom, and Knowledge. Keep it with you always, learn of its many powers, and be the leader you were always intended to be. It is life to you, and woe be unto those who try to use its' powers which are reserved for you alone. Be courageous, lead wisely with truth and kindness, and all will be well."

At that precise moment, none of the Saints would ever remember when or how it happened, a ring appeared on Jojo's right ring finger—the fit was perfect.

"To you Hooch," the Eno went on, "the unquestioned Saint of physical power, we give the Belt of Nosmas. Wear it always, as its powers are great. Its powers rest in your faith in the Eno. As you believe, so shall your powers go; powers that will increase your strength to that of a hundred, if only you believe. No mortal or immortal being will be able to withstand your strength. No one can remove the Belt from your being. You alone have that power. Terror and pain will be the result of those that defy you on your mission for the Eno. The Belt of Nosmas is meant for you and you alone. Wear it well."

And, as with Jojo's ring, the Belt of Nosmas appeared around Hooch's waist. And it, too, was a perfect fit.

"And you, Jill, lone daughter of the Saints, we confirm the gift that has already been bestowed upon you," said the Eno, as she reached into her pocket for the leaf from the Tree of Life.

"Care for this Leaf of Life," the Eno Continued, "as only in your hands will the power it possesses be unleashed. Learn of its powers, and use it in your battle against the evil that awaits you and your fellow Saints. It has the power of life. Never give any part of it away, unless in healing, both physically and of the mind. In any other's hands, the Leaf will lead to confusion, discord and eventual death. As your faith in the Eno goes, so goes your power in the use of the Leaf of Life."

And with that, Jojo, Hooch and Jill found themselves marveling at the gifts given them by the Eno. They were humbled and joyful, frightened yet fearless, and all at once overcome with emotion. But above all else, they were ready for the flight home, and the battle to be fought!

"And now the time has come for you to go," said the Eno. "Time is short. Evil is on the prowl, roaring like a lion. Trust one another. Watch over each other. Take care of your gifts. Fight the good fight. Leave nothing behind. Lay all on the line for the Eno, and all will be well."

And, in the blink of an eye, a blinding bolt of lightening exploded before them. The Saints covered their eyes, as King Mai the Omni, the Voice from within the cloud bellowed out, "*Listen and obey my Son*; *abide by the comfort and guidance of the Dove, and all will be well!*"

And then there was quiet. The Saints' eyes cleared as they looked up to see Lord Nos on the Throne, with Prince Tirips the Dove perched, as before, behind Him. Then in an instant, Prince Tirips flew from his perch next to the Saints, and grew to His previous gigantic size. Master Cherub motioned the Saints aboard. The time to depart had come.

The Flight Home

As the Saints boarded the Dove, Lord Nos gave some last words of encouragement. "May the grace and power of the Eno keep and protect you," He said. "And remember that the Eno will be with you always."

Those were the last words that Lord Nos spoke, as Prince Tirips' powerful wings jettisoned them down the steps of the Throne of the Eno, on a course following the River of Life back to the Northern Gate.

On the journey home, there was very little conversation between the Saints. They were too content on just soaking in every moment. The thought of leaving such a magnificent place and the immense task before them was foremost on their minds. The trip to the Northern Gate ended quickly. As with many journeys, the road back takes less time than the road there, or so it seemed. The Trees of Life sped by them, as did the Great Northern Gate that without a word or command given began to open.

Once through the Gate, Judah, the powerful guardian bowed and saluted the Dove and His passenger's farewell. Kebatha, Captain of the Woe-Birds, had just returned. He was ready and waiting to escort them home.

"*Farewell, my Prince*! *Go in the grace of the Eno*!" exclaimed Judah, as they flew through the gate and into the darkness of the High Heavens.

Prince Tirips turned, hovering momentarily, and gave a respectful nod back at Judah, then began the flight home. Captain Kebatha, riding his powerful Woe-Bird, Keba, led the way. Time was of the essence; a speedy trip home imperative. The evil of earth was growing.

After what seemed hours, the Saints found themselves, as they had on the trip to the Celestial City, sleepy. The smooth rhythmic motion of the Dove's wings once again, as during the journey there, caused a drowsiness to overcome them. Though they fought it, the battle to stay awake was lost. Soon, they were all fast asleep. The next thing they knew, it was time for breakfast. The door to Room 7 opened abruptly, as the Morning Duty Priest made his usual gruff announcement:

"*Everybody up*! *Breakfast in ten minutes*!"

Bob and Lou bounced out of bed, while Hooch just rolled over, pulled his pillow over his head, and continued snoring. Jojo moaned once or twice, yawned, and called out to Hooch. "Hey, Hooch, wake up!"

He continued calling him, and finally told the twins to get him up. They flew out of bed and jumped on his head.

"Owwww! Okay! Okay! I surrender! I'm up!" he screamed, grabbing both the boys, and tickling them mercilessly. "That'll teach you!"

The twins quickly escaped his grasp and climbed back up on their beds still laughing and gasping for air. Hooch and Jojo smiled at the twins, and then glanced at each other, each appearing to want to talk, but each deciding against it. For a few moments, an uneasy quiet permeated the room.

"Hey, Jojo?" asked Hooch, feeling he couldn't contain his need to talk any longer. "I had the weirdest dream last night."

But Jojo wasn't listening. He was staring: first at his watch, and then the calendar on the wall. He was wondering what day it was.

"Today's the seventh, isn't it?" he asked.

"Ahhhh, yeah," said Hooch, looking over at him in a curious sort of way, before calling out to Gus. "Hey Gus, I think Jojo is losing it, man. He wants to know…"

But before he could finish, he noticed something else that was wrong. Gus' bed was empty.

"Where's Gus!?" yelled Hooch, jumping out of his bed and running out of the room to check if maybe he'd gone down the hall to the bathroom.

When Hooch got back, Jojo had moved and was standing over Gus' bed.

"He wasn't in the bathroom, was he?" asked Jojo, looking up at Hooch. He asked it in a way that meant he already knew the answer.

"No," said Hooch quietly. "He wasn't."

"You know that dream you were going to tell me about?" ask Jojo.

"Yeah…what about it?" asked Hooch, moving closer to Gus' bed.

"I had one, too," said Jojo. "And guess what?"

"What?" asked Hooch staring blankly down at Gus' bed.

"It wasn't a dream." Jojo reminded Hooch about what Master Cherub told them about time.

"Yeah," said Hooch, "I remember. He said we could be in the Heavens for hours, days, weeks, and there might be occasions where no time at all would pass on earth."

"Which is exactly what happened," answered Jojo. He then held up his left hand exposing a ring that wasn't there when he went to bed the night before.

"Remember?" he said to Hooch, as they both stared at the ring.

"Yeah, I remember," said Hooch, smiling at Jojo as he lifted up his shirt exposing the Belt of Nosmas that had been given to him. "Do you?"

Both boys smiled and nodded their heads. It was confirmed. What happened last night really did take place; it wasn't a dream. No time had passed at all and nothing was different; or was it?

"This is the same day that we spent the morning in the cafeteria having breakfast discussing the plan to run away. Remember? The exact same day, only…"

"Only what?" asked Hooch. "*What*?"

"Only you didn't have that belt, and I never had this ring! And Gus was still in his bed," continued Jojo.

Everything, as much as could be expected, made sense; except for Gus.

"He should be in his bed," said Hooch. "How could everything be the same, and Gus not be here? It just doesn't make sense."

"I don't know," mumbled Jojo. "I just don't know."

"What about Jill? We need to make sure she's all right!" shouted Hooch. "Let's get over to her room. We've still got a few minutes before the chow line forms to the cafeteria."

"We can't," said Jojo. "If we're caught, we'll end up in the Hole for a week! And besides, she wasn't lost to the Underlings, like Gus was, *before* we made the journey. That's the difference. She was with us the entire time. I'm sure she made it just like we did. "

"I'll believe it when I see her!" said Hooch. "Now, I'm going with or without you!"

As Jojo tried to block Hooch from going, there was a knock on the door.

"Don't answer it!" yelled Jojo. "It's probably the Morning Duty Priest. Or worse, it could be the *It*."

Hooch just kept moving. "Get out of the way, JoJo. I don't care who it is. And I don't want to hurt you. But I will." But before Hooch was forced to do something he dreaded, the door started to open. The boys froze. Slowly, as it opened, Jill poked her head in.

"Hi guys," she said in a soft, nervous voice. "Can I come in?"

"Yes!" shouted Hooch pulling her inside, quickly closing the door behind her, and giving her a big hug.

"I had to talk to you, guys. Something just popped into my head telling me to get over here right away. And I have to tell you, not only that, but I had the weirdest…" but she stopped suddenly unable to finish her thought. Something else caught her attention, "Hey, where's Gus?"

Both Hooch and Jojo looked at each other, neither of them wanting to speak. Finally, Jojo did.

"He's gone," he said. "We've looked everywhere."

"Then it *is* true!" shouted Jill as her eyes began to tear up at the sight of Gus' empty bed. She pulled a leaf, the Leaf of Life from one pocket of her jacket with one hand, and a Dove's feather from the other. "It *wasn't* a dream!"

Hooch immediately showed her the belt around his waist, and Jojo showed her his ring.

"What does it all mean?" asked Jill, as she noticed both Hooch and Jojo looking in the direction of their window. The same window they had escaped from the night before.

"I believe that we are about to find out," said Hooch.

Jojo was already making his way across the room to the window where a Dove of exquisite beauty had alighted on the windowsill. Hooch opened the window and was glad he did.

"Prince Tirips!" he shouted. "Is it really you?"

"Good day to you, oh, sons and daughter of earth!" said Prince Tirips. "Yes, it is really me, and I'm so glad to once again be amongst the Eno's beloved 31st Street Saints!"

After many deep bows of reverence and a tear or two of joy, the Saints gathered themselves as close to the Dove as possible. His appearance comforted them. It also meant there was news from Lord Nos.

"Lord Nos knows that evil will soon be upon you, and he desires that you be prepared," began the Prince. "Listen carefully to what must take place. You will soon be taken from here and locked away for a time, as it is the will of the Eno. It will be harsh and uncomfortable. But you must never give up. Be of great courage, and remain faithful, and all will be well. I will return."

"Locked away?" asked Jill. "But…why? We haven't done anything."

As the words left her mouth, the Prince called out, "The evil is upon you!"

The door to Room 7 swung open, as the *It* stormed in and gave the command to, "Seize them and escort them to the Hole!" Two hooded Priests took the Saints by the arms and led them out of the room and off to the Hole, as the *It* bellowed, "You know the rules! No females may cross over to the male dorms! Ten days in the Hole!"

The Saints looked back to see if Prince Tirips was still there, but he was gone. Their hearts sank as the Priests escorted them down to the basement of the orphanage to the cold, dank prison known as the Hole. The steel door of the Hole was opened, and the Saints were thrown inside.

"Enjoy your stay," mocked the *It*, as the hooded beast then turned towards Jojo. "And as for you, this just means a temporary delay until we celebrate *your* birthday. But don't fear, we *will* celebrate it soon enough!" An unbearable, putrid smelling stench of liquor and onions burst forth from beneath the hooded black robe, as chilling evil laughter filled the Hole. "And we may include your two friends in *their* early celebration, as well."

The door of the Hole slammed shut. Each Saint shuffled over to lie on an old rusty cot, one of many that lined the walls of the Hole. They plopped down, disheartened and discouraged, on a razor thin mattress with springs poking through. As best they could, they curled up with the one thin blanket allotted to warm them, with only an elbow to rest their weary heads. It wasn't even night yet, and the chill was almost unbearable. Hooch was the first to speak.

"I can't believe that Prince Tirips didn't do anything. He just deserted us. He said He would always be there for us!"

"He also said to be of great courage and that he would return," said Jill. "We mustn't give up so easily."

"Jill is right," added Jojo. "If it is the will of the Eno that we wait here in the Hole, then so be it; we wait. Prince Tirips said he would return. So until he does, we wait."

Hooch just shook his head. He was too cold, uncomfortable, depressed and discouraged to put up any other arguments. Instead, he rolled over, as did Jojo and Jill, and went silent. Breakfast, lunch, and dinner, a veritable smorgasbord of stale bread and water, came and went in silence on that first infamous day in the Hole.

The silence among them was almost as unbearable as the Hole itself. No more words were spoken. Night fell quickly, and the cold grew in intensity. Each Saint did their best to warm themselves. Thoughts of what was to happen next racked their brains. Questions flooded their minds. Had the Eno deserted them? Would the Prince really return? Had they failed in their task before it even began? Or, worst of all, would they all end up like the Underlings? A voice cut through their thoughts like a hot knife through butter. It was Jojo.

"We must remember, Prince Tirips gave us the warning from Lord Nos that we were to be put in a very harsh and uncomfortable place for a time," he said, the words shivering through his teeth. "This is that place. He said not to give up. So we won't. We must trust. We must."

And then, after speaking those words, there once again, was silence.